None are ignorant to the Reaper's heart.

And so, no one would find it odd if the eastern front's Headless Reaper would, on occasion or even frequently, celebrate his youth.

86—EIGHTY-SIX

Alter.1

ASATO ASATO

Translation by Roman Lempert
Cover art by Shirabii

Yen On
150 West 30th Street, 19th Floor
New York, NY 10001

Visit us at yenpress.com

facebook.com/yenpress
twitter.com/yenpress

yenpress.tumblr.com
instagram.com/yenpress

First Yen On Edition: September 2024
Edited by Yen On Editorial: Payton Campbell
Designed by Yen Press Design: Liz Parlett

Library of Congress Cataloging-in-Publication Data
Names: Asato, Asato, author. | Lempert, Roman, translator. | Shirabii, artist.
Title: 86—eighty-six alter / Asato Asato ; translation by Roman Lempert ; cover art by Shirabii.
Other titles: 86—eighty-six. English
Description: New York : Yen On, 2024.
Identifiers: LCCN 2024023269 | ISBN 9781975392703 (trade paperback)
Subjects: CYAC: Science fiction. | Soldiers—Fiction. | LCGFT: Science fiction. | War fiction. | Light novels.
Classification: LCC PZ7.1.A79 A24 2024 | DDC [Fic]—dc23
LC record available at https://lccn.loc.gov/2024023269

ISBNs: 978-1-9753-9270-3 (paperback)
978-1-9753-9271-0 (ebook)

10 9 8 7 6 5 4 3 2 1

LSC-C

Printed in the United States of America

86

[EIGHTY-SIX]

Life, land, and legacy.
All reduced to a number.

Alter. 1

THE REAPER'S OCCASIONAL ADOLESCENCE

ASATO ASATO

ILLUSTRATION: Shirabii

MECHANICAL DESIGN: I-IV

86

[EIGHTY-SIX]

They spent their adolescence there,
on the battlefield.

THE REPUBLIC OF SAN MAGNOLIA ARC

They spent their adolescence there, on the battlefield.

[EIGHTY-SIX]

Life, land, and legacy.
All reduced to a number.

86 ALTER VOLUME ONE

86

EIGHTY-
SIX

THE REPUBLIC OF SAN MAGNOLIA ARC

Two Contours on a Winter Day

Powder snow lay over the market in Liberté et Égalité's revolution square, glittering in the soft sunlight of winter. There was a bazaar being held for the upcoming Atonement Festival. It was a fire festival for forgiveness held yearly before the coming of spring, but with the passage of time the original meaning of the festival had faded, and it was now simply seen as one more yearly event.

As she was walking through the bazaar filled with the excitement of a coming holiday, an eleven-year-old Lena stopped in her tracks. As everyone went about the place accompanied by friends, family, or lovers, Lena seemed to be the only one walking alone. She had no romantic relationships, her father died when she was young, and her mother loathed going out to such vulgar, public places. Since Lena skipped grades repeatedly, she had only one friend her age.

It was perhaps unavoidable, then, that she would be here all alone.

After all, she spent every waking moment ardently pursuing the goal of becoming a soldier so she could someday live up to the words of the person who saved her life. She never lamented that choice…but at times like these, there was a pinch of regret.

She looked up at the clear winter sky, so different from the sky she beheld on that fateful day. Was my savior still out there, fighting beneath the same sky? Had he been able to reunite with the brother he longs to meet? Even for a fleeting moment?

Those words alone left her lips, cooled by the winter wind, as she looked up at the azure sky stretching out into the battlefield.

There was little hope of finding a shovel lying around in those long-abandoned city ruins. With the skeleton so stripped of flesh, there was little concern of animals picking away at the corpse. It also meant that the grave he wanted to dig wouldn't need to be very deep, but even so, digging through the cold ground with nothing but a bayonet was backbreaking work—Shin only being twelve and still very short in stature only made it harder.

If Fido hadn't come looking for him and helped out, it would have surely taken him the whole day. He was somehow able to finish before sundown. He leaned against Fido, whom he used to shield himself from the wind, as he stood in front of the modest mound of soil and sipped on some hot water he had melted from snow.

The Eighty-Six weren't allowed to have grave markers, and no flowers grew in the snow-laden ruins for him to place by the grave. The sky was a clear blue, a far cry from the snowfall of the night prior, but there wasn't another soul around. Shin had no words to direct to his brother, now reduced to a bleached skeleton.

After all, even if he buried his brother's remains here, his ghost was elsewhere.

His bayonet's tip was bent out of shape after digging through ground as cold and hard as steel for a whole day. He held up the piece of his brother's Juggernaut's armor which had been scavenged by Fido, using it to block off the sunlight. Drawn on the feeble aluminum alloy armor, too thin to even block machine gun fire, was the Personal Mark of a headless, skeletal knight.

A ghost with its head cut off that refused to stay dead.

That Personal Mark felt like a sarcastic jab at Shin himself, but any chance he had of ever knowing why his brother drew it on his unit was gone forever.

While keeping the container Shin was leaning against still, Fido swerved its optical sensor around and blinked its round lens once.

"*...Pi.*"

"No, they won't worry even if I don't go back right away. The head of maintenance can't stand me anyway."

Shin cracked a self-deprecating smile as he thought back to the young head of maintenance for his squadron's base. Shin didn't think he was a bad guy. It was because he cared for Processors ten years younger than him that he couldn't tolerate the "Reaper" that drove everyone around him to their deaths.

The squad captain, who had been friends with the head of maintenance ever since their time in the internment camps and seemed to care a lot for Shin as the youngest of the group, also died in combat last night.

And so did all his squad mates. Again.

There was no one waiting for him to come back. No one had expected him to survive, or even wished for that to begin with. Still, he knew he had to survive. Even at times like these, there was the faint desire to cling to life.

As he looked up to the azure sky, which his brother's remains had gazed at to the bitter end, he whispered while knowing no one was there to concur or disagree with him.

With over a hundred kilometers of wall between Liberté et Égalité and the battlefield, reinforced by the Gran Mur, minefields, and jamming, the two couldn't possibly reach each other. And so...

In one corner of the street where the people uplifted by the festivities wouldn't notice her, she looked up at the eastern sky which oversaw the battlefield.

"...It's cold."

* * *

In one corner of an abandoned battlefield, in ruins blocked by the snow, he looked up to the western sky, where the sun would set.

"...It's cold, isn't it?"

Neither of them could know that, at that moment, they were linked through gazes that met and words that slipped from their lips, frozen and white into the air.

August 25th (Raiden's Birthday)

"Isn't it your birthday today?"

Raiden frowned at the sudden question. It'd been over a year since he began his torturous life in the Eighty-Sixth Sector. And that was also how long he'd known this unpleasant Reaper captain of his, who'd asked such an out-of-place question.

But thinking about it now, it was true. He turned thirteen today. And so had Shin.

"Y-yeah. Now that you mention it."

He'd forgotten, since no one celebrated birthdays here at the Eighty-Sixth Sector. There was no need to remember dates of birth, either. But Raiden then realized something and asked, not that a few months' difference would make him consider Shin to be his elder.

"What about yours?"

"I forgot," he replied indifferently.

He wasn't being evasive about it; he just honestly didn't remember, and his tone implied that the fact he forgot didn't hurt him. In a few years, he would be told he was born in May, but neither of them had any way of knowing that now, of course.

Shin finally cocked his head a little and said, "Why not celebrate it?"

"...I guess it's not a bad idea."

Much like how Shin indifferently admitted to forgetting his own birthday, most of their squad mates didn't remember their dates of birth.

They couldn't recall much from the time before they were cast into the Eighty-Sixth Sector—they were burned by the fires of war.

But Raiden happened to remember his, so maybe this wouldn't be a terrible idea.

And besides.

"So, why are you really doing this?"

"It's almost time this unit got reorganized, so I figured it would be a good excuse to unwind with the surviving members."

Yeah, that was about what Raiden thought. He glared at Shin a little, but he didn't mind.

"It looks like the Legion won't be moving for the next day or two, and we got a bunch of sugar the other day, so maybe we could make something sweet," Shin said, and cracked an unpleasant smirk.

Raiden got a really bad feeling.

"We also got some canned crackers and milk cans from the emergency storehouse, and we've got eggs. I brought over a recipe book I found, so maybe we—and by we, I mean I—could make a custard cake."

"Okay, no."

Shin was a terrible cook. Raiden didn't know for sure if it was because he was too impatient and skipped steps, measured everything by eye, or because he regarded cooking with a notable lack of delicacy, never caring for how strong the fire was and letting the pot boil over.

Either way, he was simply too rough to cook properly. And he probably cared nothing for taste, either.

Shin was still smirking for some reason. "No need to be shy."

"I ain't shy, I just feel like I'm in danger here… Dammit."

Realizing he was being teased, Raiden scratched his head. It had been a year since they met. At the time he'd thought this guy was a cold, heartless angel of death. And while Shin had learned how to smile, Raiden wasn't sure how to feel about Shin's attempts at teasing him.

"If you just want to eat sweets you could just say so. Fine. I'll make it."

Crushing crackers to make tart batter and stuffing it full of custard cream. That much should be doable even in the poor conditions of the

Eighty-Sixth Sector, though they would perhaps have to improvise an oven somehow.

Still, Shin demanding sweets now meant he really was a kid deep down, Raiden thought with a hint of surprise as he glanced at him

Shin, however, gazed back with a puzzled expression.

"That's not it… I don't like sweets."

"Asshole."

Lena + Annette

"We're both going to be soldiers starting tomorrow, you know? Let's use our last day of freedom to go shopping."

And so, at Anette's invitation, Lena went with her to Liberté et Égalité's city center, to the First Sector's biggest department store.

"You're exaggerating, Annette. We're not going to live in the barracks or anything."

"Oh, don't be such a stick in the mud. Who can pass off a good excuse to go shopping?"

Annette looked altogether thrilled, her handbag swinging over her arm. Lena trailed after her with a smile.

The store manager spotted two high-class young ladies approaching and walked over to personally greet and show them around, but the two politely turned them away and stopped by whichever stores caught their eye.

Gaudy, high-class dresses that were the current craze, shoes, jewelry, assorted sweets. Everything was vivid and brilliant, making their hearts dance.

"Check this out, Lena! It's got to be this white-and-gold one! Try it on, come on!"

"Ah, wait. In that case, Annette, you gotta try on the lacy one over there. It'll look great on you."

"…Don't you think these heels are a little too tall?"

"Don't worry about that, Lena. It looks mature and cool."

* * *

"Annette, look! This necklace and earring set is so cute!"

"I-I think I'll pass on that. I'm not good with stuff that's red like blood. Maybe I'll go for this one. Same design, but it's blue."

"...Lena, did you decide which one you want? They're recommending both the forêt-noire and the rouge."

"...Not yet. Hey, since today's special, maybe we can get both?"

They spent the days cheerfully combing through the department store before carrying their shopping bags to a café on the top floor. The store manager appeared seemingly out of nowhere, saying he could have the bags delivered to their mansions, and took them off the girls' hands.

They were led to the best seat in the café: a spot by a window that offered them a scenic view to enjoy with their tea and coffee. Lena was more of a tea person while Annette insisted on coffee. Both were synthetized products made in mass-production factories, so no amount of careful brewing would recreate the flavor of the real things as they remembered.

The eight main streets spread from the radial plaza and stretched into the suburbs. The streets were beautiful, well-maintained, and classy. For scenery preservation, the Republic restricted the number of stories buildings could have, so the view from this rooftop café in a building with unrestricted height was completely unobstructed. As she watched the sunset over Liberté et Égalité, Annette spoke up.

"...You said you want to be a Handler, right, Lena?"

"Yes. My post's already been decided."

"You're really such a weirdo."

Annette's posting was, naturally, for the research division. She was taking over her late father's research.

A strange thought came to mind, and Lena's hands stopped halfway through raising the teacup to her lips. Their time as girls having fun on the town was up. Come tomorrow, they'll be setting foot into the world of grown-ups a bit earlier than girls their age… They'll be joining the world of the military.

She hung her head and smiled.

"Thank you for today. I'm glad I came along. I mean, we'll be busy starting tomorrow."

"Right? But hey, if you want to hang out, feel free to drop by the lab."

"Is that all right?"

"You're always welcome as far as I'm concerned, Lena."

Annette remembered something, put down her coffee, and leaned in. She lowered her voice like she was sharing some special secret.

"I saw the cutest mugs in the store downstairs. Matching mugs, with black-and-white rabbits. Let's get those. We can put them in my lab, and that'll be your designated mug. And you've got to come over if you've got your own mug, right?"

Seeing her friend's eyes light up like a child's, Lena couldn't help but giggle. She leaned in and whispered back.

"Of course, Annette."

My precious best friend.

Claymore Squadron

"So long as you understand. Don't worry, I'll clear this up."

"…Sorry."

"Don't beat yourself up over it. Just rest."

Saying this, Raiden Shuga—vice captain of the 28th ward's first defensive squadron, Claymore—rose from a creaking wooden chair. He made to leave this shabby, prefabricated barracks room and return to his own, but paused and turned around.

"And don't join the Resonance even if the situation changes, you hear me? Having you Resonate when you're all frazzled just makes it harder for us, Shin!"

Confirming that Shin feebly stuck a hand out of the blanket and waved in a show of consent, Raiden closed the door behind him. He entered the hangar to prepare for a sortie, where he saw his surprisingly few remaining squad mates peering at him. The mortality rate of Processors was exceedingly high, so most squadrons had to fight with numbers that didn't meet the usual criteria.

But this time the vacancies weren't due to casualties. It had been getting colder over the last few days, and a few of their members came down with a cold, including their captain, Shin. Even the oldest in the squadron were in their late teens, so their bodies weren't fully developed yet. Between that and the terrible living conditions, disease outbreaks weren't uncommon during winter.

Raiden didn't let his concern show on his face. Having the newer, more unreliable members get taken out of commission was one thing, but Shin and Daiya being down for the count was a significant blow. Still, this squadron was doing better than most. It had plenty of veterans, meaning they could tell the sick to rest and recover. Most other squadrons had to send their sick and injured out to fight while knowing they were in no condition to do so, which was essentially a death sentence. Indeed, most people forced to fight when they could rarely come back from those sorties.

Raiden saw one of the newer boys frown in concern.

"...Can we really do it this time...? I mean, the cap'n's not here..."

Theo chuckled and said they wouldn't be much safer with Shin here, though he wasn't being mean. Kurena, who was closer to Theo in age, regarded him with a miffed expression.

Anju, the boy's platoon captain, smiled softly.

"I know you're a bit spoiled, Rito, so let me give you this fair warning... If you're going to blindly rely on Shin in battle, you'll end up dead."

Rito's eyes widened in surprise. He relied on their captain to no end in these battles.

"All his instructions and warnings are subject to priorities based on the situation. He can't always help you. Only those who look at the state of battle themselves, make their own judgment calls, and rely on no one survive. Plus... You know. Neither we nor Shin will always be there to be your babysitters."

Rito's prepubescent face hardened as he recalled their reality. The battlefield they were on was a place where everyone died sooner or later. He looked like he was about to burst into tears, but Raiden ruffled his short, agate colored hair. This was something Rito was used to, and it didn't come as a surprise.

"We can make it just fine with today's numbers… No one's planning on letting anyone die here. And that guy, he might act like he doesn't care, but he does."

Enough that Raiden had to repeatedly warn Shin not to Resonate while he was sick.

Like they said during the briefing, they all returned from that day's battle safely. When Raiden saw Shin get out of bed early to check on them, Raiden frowned at him.

"I told you to stay in bed."

"I'm feeling better. Plus, I figured you'd prefer to hear the bad news sooner rather than later."

True to his words, Shin seemed to have gotten enough sleep and the color had mostly returned to his face, but he still looked relatively bad. Raiden repressed the urge to point that out and remained silent.

"Bad news?"

"They sent over our next posting."

Looking around he saw Daiya, who was also sick that day. The usually mirthful look in his blue eyes was now cold and hard. The Processors's postings in each sector were roughly six months long to prevent them from conspiring together and stoking rebellions. After six months, squadrons were dissolved, and their troops were scattered and reorganized into other squadrons. This squadron was entering its fifth month, so getting their next posting wasn't unusual, but…

Raiden looked down at Shin, who gazed back at him and said with his usual unyielding, indifferent tone, "All platoon leaders, me included, are to be sent to the first defensive ward's first defensive unit."

Rito gasped. Raiden squinted his eyes suspiciously. The first ward's first defensive unit.

"...Spearhead, huh?"

The eastern front was the most contested and fierce battlefield, and Spearhead was the squadron charged with manning its first line of defense.

It was the front that claimed the most lives in this battlefield with no casualties.

It was brief and ever so faint, but Raiden certainly saw it—their captain, bearer of the title of "Reaper," flashing a dreadful, cold smile.

Daiya + Anju

"I heard it meowing in a house that got blasted by a Löwe shell, and my eyes met his. It was through the sensor, but we talked, heart-to-heart."

With an expression fitting the cheapest, most pulpy tragedy known to man, Daiya held a black kitten with white legs up to his chest. Its triangular ears and silvery whiskers twitched as it meowed in what was indeed a very distinctive voice.

"I looked around and found another cat, probably its mother or something, crushed under the rubble. And look at how tiny it is! There's no way this little guy can make it on its own."

Forced to play along with these theatrics while filling out a supply order form, Shin moved his emotionless crimson eyes to Daiya. Shin had been wondering why Daiya had opened his canopy and exposed himself to danger before the battle was over, even if there were no Legion in the vicinity. And this kitten was the reason.

What's more, Shin could see where this was going. He was already scanning the desk for the heaviest object he could reach for.

"I promise I'll take good care of it...so please let me keep it, Mom!"

As soon as he heard that last word, Shin picked up a sheathed bayonet knife sitting on the table and tossed it at Daiya. Expecting this, Daiya jerked his neck to dodge...only to take a direct hit in the forehead from the paperweight Shin tossed next. Daiya's head wobbled back.

The kitten hopped out of his arms, and Anju caught it in the heat of the moment, hugging it to her chest.

"Good read on his joke, Shin," she said.

"Anju… I'm begging you: worry about me in this situation, not it…"

The cat meowed in Anju's arms, as if to say *No one cares about that.*

"I'll go wash the kitten, then. Remember those rags we got when we asked for towels, Shin? I'll be taking one of those."

"Sure."

Anju walked out, the kitten in her arms, and Daiya got back to his feet, quick to recover in more ways than one. Seeing Shin reach for an old, leather-bound book with a metallic fixture on its spine, he knew better than to repeat the bad joke.

"So, can we keep it?"

"I don't mind," Shin replied with indifference, but Daiya brought a hand to his forehead, shaking his head in a show of sorrow.

"Aaah, no, Shin, that's not how it goes! You're supposed to tell us to put it back where we found it! Right?!"

"…"

"And then I try really hard to persuade you with tears in my eyes, and promise I'll look after it, and then you'll go, *Oh fine, have it your way!* Got it? Let's try it one more time from the top…"

"We can start over and I can tell you that, but if I do, you really will have to go put it back where you found it. Without your Juggernaut."

Today's combat area was quite far from here on foot, and there were still Ameise and self-propelled mines prowling about, but Shin wasn't about to care about that.

Sensing from Shin's indifferent tone that he was being serious, Daiya fell silent, his hands still spread. Shin let out a deep sigh.

Seriously, this guy.

Theo + Kaie + Haruto + Fido

"And when I looked really carefully, I saw it. Lots of green lights floating above the river…"

"Whoaaaaaa, stop iiiit…!"

"…!"

As Shin came back from pouring himself a fresh cup of coffee, he spotted Kaie screaming and clinging to Haruto like he was some kind of stuffed toy, with Theo right behind her, whispering something in an amused manner. Apparently, the Handler girl on the other side of the Resonance reacted much the same way as Kaie.

Thunder rumbled outside. It was a rainy night, making it the perfect time for scary stories. Shin wasn't sure if this weather extended to the First Sector, where the Handler was, though.

"That river's been the site of many a battle over the years, so the ghosts of ancient soldiers sensed our battle and awoke from their eternal slumber…"

"I said stop it, Theo, you moroooon!"

If anything, those were probably fireflies.

As Kaie screamed, the Handler was apparently petrified into silence. Shin let that thought cross his mind and decided against saying it. Cutting into Theo's prank felt like it was more trouble than it was worth.

It certainly wasn't because the way the Handler girl curled up and trembled like a scared rabbit was funny. Certainly not. As Kaie hugged Haruto tightly until he went slightly pale—from asphyxiation—Haruto smirked.

"Oh, I saw one like this, too," he said. "This black shadow standing in the woods. I looked away from it this one time, and when I looked back, it was closer. Then I looked away again, and when I looked back it was even closer…"

"Whaaaaaaaaaaaaaa!"

"Ugh!"

Why do you have to say things that literally tighten the noose on you?

Shin let that thought cross his mind and decided against saying it. He noticed Theo, his hands placed on the chair's backrest and his chin resting on them, glance at him.

"Good timing, Undertaker. You have any ghost stories to share?"

"No… Not really."

"Bummer."

Theo scoffed in disappointment at Shin's immediate denial, but then Shin remembered and looked back at the stairs he just walked up. It wasn't a ghost story per se, but…

"By the way, who was that outside the landing's window? They can't be cleaning the windows in this rain."

"Hold up!" Kaie, Haruto, and Theo all shouted at once.

Shin raised an eyebrow. "…What's gotten into you three?"

"Don't act all incredulous on us! What you said is weird! Like, all sorts of weird!"

"Like you said, nobody's crazy enough to go outside in this rain, and if they're *outside* the window of the landing between the first and second floor, where would they be standing?! What are they, flying?!"

"I mean, you just came from the dining hall! There wasn't anyone there, was there?!"

Come to think of it, that was true.

"So maybe it's someone who isn't alive."

"Cut it out!"

They all shouted at Shin as loud as they could, which forced him to go quiet. Theo, Haruto, and Kaie all started rubbing their forearms excitedly.

"Oh, come on, Undertaker. So you *do* have a horror story!"

"I guess he's just too used to it and horror doesn't register as scary for him! Wait, so how many horror stories have you gone through?!"

"I'm scared! I guess Undertaker really did end up being the scariest person here!"

Over the background of their squealing, Shin thought he could hear the Handler girl fall over, apparently having reached the limits of what she could put up with.

On his way back from picking up reusable parts, Fido stopped in its tracks upon hearing all the noise from the second floor. Its container was filled with large metallic statues it found lying inside a building that collapsed during battle a few days ago. The polished silver statues were quite beautiful, apparently fashioned after great men and heroes, but a few of them were a bit tilted from when Fido accidentally hit the barracks building.

It blinked its optical sensor once and then continued on its way back to the automatic factory's recycling furnace. It threw the statues along with the other reusable parts into the furnace and, after praising itself for a day of work well done, the diligent Scavenger returned to its designated standby space.

Raiden + Kurena

"...This is both cruel *and* unusual, if you ask me..."

Since Eighty-Six didn't count as human, they wouldn't be given proper food, shelter, or clothing, and so the Processors' field uniforms and the storehouses that housed them were covered in dust from years of neglect. Worse yet, the uniforms themselves were worn out from overuse and effectively useless.

This meant the Processors needed to pick up certain skills to get by, and some people were naturally more proficient at them than others.

"Wait, I never knew you were good at mending clothes," Raiden said, seated by the table with his cheek resting on his hand.

"I dunno. Am I?" Shin asked while mending the frayed sleeve of a uniform.

Given how haphazard and bad he was with cooking, it only seemed reasonable to assume he'd be bad with work as precise as sewing. Raiden was always a bit baffled by the fact that he defied this logic, but Shin didn't seem to mind.

Kurena sat next to them, dangling her legs like a little girl as she waited for Shin to finish working on the uniform, and Raiden was honestly fed up with her, too. Yes, Shin wasn't fixing his own uniform here.

"I mean, come on. You're not a kid anymore. Fix your own clothes, Kurena."

"I'm bad at patching clothes." Kurena looked away from Raiden in a huff.

What she said wasn't quite precise. She wasn't just bad at sewing—she was catastrophically inept. To illustrate why her lack of ability had to be described as catastrophic, back when they were first assigned to the same unit, she was so terrible at it that when Shin saw her try, he snatched up her entire uniform set and said he'd do it instead.

He didn't do it out of some gentlemanly impulse to keep a girl from hurting her hands trying to sew the rough fabric of the field uniform. It was because her hands were completely bloodied, and he didn't want her to waste any more string.

So ever since, whenever her clothes got torn, she'd come to Shin for help—though she never brought any underwear. This could be seen as her fawning on him, he supposed. Or some moving attempt on her behalf to talk to him. But from Raiden's perspective as an onlooker, this was why Shin would never see Kurena as a girl, but only as a troublesome little sister.

"...Major, what do you think about what Kurena just said?"

Shin turned the conversation to Lena, who was Resonating with him but kept silent out of consideration while he worked. For some reason, she didn't answer, which made Raiden open one eye.

"What's wrong?"

Lena remained quiet for another long moment, before gingerly speaking up.

"Erm... What's 'patching'...?"

Silence hung over them, and then, they all sighed. Hard.

"I knew you were a rich princess, but holy hell..."

"Whoa... I mean, there's no way you're that oblivious, right?"

"Major, you're one of those people, aren't you? The kind who can't even sew a button."

Another pause.

"...Sewing...buttons? Aren't you supposed to close buttons?"

Apparently, she never saw a button come off before. She must have had very capable maids working at her mansion or something.

"Don't tell me you've never had to thread a needle?"

"...Thread, a needle...?"

The very basics of sewing were lost on her, it seemed. Shin sighed again, taken aback, and Lena very clearly became flustered. Kurena, on the other hand, huffed out proudly.

"Even I can manage that much, Major," she said.

"Huuuh?! Is not knowing that something people should be ashamed of?! Is it, Major Nouzen?!"

Shin said nothing, likely because he and Raiden had the same exasperated thought cross their minds.

Talk about the pot calling the kettle black.

Shin + Lena

"...Mm."

Feeling a light weight lean against his arm, he looked down. Kurena, who he remembered was busy playing with the cat earlier, was now leaning against him, asleep. Shin nimbly opened his bookmarked book with one hand and remained silent for a moment. Kurena was sleeping contently, her breathing serene. Looking at her now, he truly felt like she hadn't matured much, if at all. Or rather, she might have grown on the outside, but not at all on the inside.

Shrugging that thought off, Shin left the girl beside him to her nap and returned to reading. Given the uncomfortable position, she'd probably wake up soon anyway, and if she didn't, he could call Anju over to pick her up.

But as he reached that conclusion, his Para-RAID activated. Lena's voice, ever a pleasant chime, greeted him as it always did.

"...Good evening, Captain Nouzen."

Oh, this is bad.

That thought reflexively shot through his mind, but then he frowned, realizing this was a weird thing to think.

...Wait, why do I think it's bad?

* * *

Apparently, the other usual members were out cleaning or something, because Shin was all alone in that room. Or so Lena thought, but as she heard a faint breathing sound that clearly didn't belong to Shin, she cocked her head curiously. It was faint… Like someone sleeping.

"…Is someone else there?"

"Well, sort of… Kurena's sleeping here."

Apparently, she was leaning on him, and he couldn't move. Imagining it made Lena giggle.

"Second Lieutenant Kukumila sounds like a cute little sister, doesn't she?"

"An oddly clingy one, at that."

His voice and tone sounded like someone stumped about how to deal with a kitten that ran into their house from the rain and refused to leave. Lena laughed out loud, imagining the sour look on his face.

But, at the same time, something deep inside her chest prickled with…irritation.

…Eh?

Once she became aware of it, the irritation instantly ballooned. Why? Why does this make her feel so irate? And it seemed Lena's wavering emotions were strong enough to be picked up by Shin on the other side of the Para-RAID.

"…Major?"

"What?"

Her voice came out so stinging and harsh that even she was taken aback by it.

"It's just… Did I upset you?"

"No."

There it is again.

"…You're upset."

"I'm not!"

Shin fell silent. Contrary to her words, Lena grabbed a nearby cushion and squished it in her arms.

Heavenly Blue in the Everlasting Dark

Despite being divested of their human rights and reduced to drone parts forced to fight the Legion on the front lines, even the Eighty-Six weren't fighting at all hours of the day.

"...Isn't that dangerous? I mean, you're walking through the contested areas all on your own..."

Lena was in her room on her family estate in the peaceful capital, far from the front lines. As she was flipping through a fireworks catalog she brought from a merchant who made fireworks to order, she spoke through the Para-RAID.

Shin, who was scouring for usable supplies in an abandoned city ruin on one corner of the battlefield, shrugged at her question.

"It's fine, there aren't any Legion in the area. You know what I mean, right?"

"Well, yes, but what about wolves, or bears, or tigers?"

"They get targeted by the Legion, too, if they run into any combat, so they avoid the contested areas where there's a lot of fighting. And they avoid humans, since they can't tell them apart from self-propelled mines."

"Besides, there aren't any tigers in this region," Shin remarked indifferently. Lena's lips perked up and into a smile. Shin seemed to notice this. Compared to when they first started talking, they now naturally discussed trifling topics like this.

"You seem like you're enjoying yourself... What are you doing right now?"

"Huh? Oh... Erm."

Coming up with an answer, she chuckled. This was still gunpowder to be fired from a tube, albeit for a different purpose.

"I'm just comparing artillery shells so I can pick out the right one."

"...And that's fun?"

"Oh, yes. I imagine you'll love it... And besides, you're not one to talk."

The Para-RAID employed the collective subconscious to transmit their voices, allowing them to subtly feel each other's emotions like they would in a face-to-face conversation. Right now, she could tell that Shin—in a departure from his usual taciturn, detached self—was clearly enjoying himself.

Apparently, he had found the entrance to some underground structure and was about to embark on a bit of an exploration mission, chemical glow stick in hand. Perhaps it was precisely because they spent their childhood in an internment camp, without any way to play and constantly dreading an uncertain tomorrow, that the Eighty-Six were so active in seeking out joy in the most trivial parts of daily life. Boys often relished exploring or finding secret bases.

And surely she wasn't imagining the way his nearly inaudible footsteps felt incredibly light, or that he was looking around actively. He was expecting to make some kind of discovery, and Lena chuckled at that thought.

"I hope you find something. Like an ancient ruin or a buried pirate treasure."

"Given we're inland, these are probably old subway ruins. I doubt I'll find anything like that."

Shin cracked a warm smile at Lena's enthusiasm, but then she felt him stop. His military boots, usually silent, let out a screech that echoed hard and far. Wherever he was now, it was very spacious.

Hundreds of kilometers away, past the Gran Mur, she heard this boy whose face she had never seen silently hold his breath.

"...It'd be nice if we could Resonate my sense of sight... If you could see what I'm seeing."

He didn't know what this place was originally for. It sank into darkness just ahead, and he couldn't tell how big it was, but it was all coated in azure dark. Part of the ceiling was a hole that seemed to extend to the surface, with the pale summer sun casting its thin beams inside.

Before him stretched a seemingly boundless underground lake of limpid water—likely from accumulated rainwater—its surface wavering ever so slightly. A marble statue of the Holy Mother, originally having decorated some other place, smiled serenely at him from within the cerulean dark.

Like a grim reaper that left no footsteps, Shin approached the edge of the quivering water's surface.

"...A far east religion says that blue is the color of the world of the dead, and all cultures see butterflies as symbols of the spirits of the dead."

The source of the blue light was the wreckage of countless Edelfalter sunken into the water, their blue butterfly wings refracting the light. Maybe they were shot down by artillery once... Or perhaps this was just where they chose to die.

Lena firmly asked him to stop. Shin had to smile at this Handler who would go so far to mourn the death of people...of Eighty-Six who weren't even human.

"Yes. I don't believe in it either... But..." Looking up, knowing full well that there was no heaven or hell out there, he narrowed his eyes in a somewhat pious manner. "I do think that if this is what you get to see before the end, maybe it's not so bad."

As the Holy Mother's sculpture drifted in the dark water, a pious smile on her lips, a single streak of white light cast a faint, silvery glow on her.

The Carious Saber's Edge

The frozen twilight battlefield was covered in blue passion flowers blooming out of season and silent as the eternal slumber of death. It was in this chilling blue that Shin snapped out of the combat heat that dominated his thoughts.

Looking around the battlefield through the veil of his optical screen, he saw no movement, no stirring. Only the smoldering wreckage of Legion lying amidst the sea of flowers, silently run aground with nary a flame billowing from them.

Look though he may, there were no enemies left—no people,

either—in this battlefield that had long since slipped from the dominion of man.

For a second, the thought crossed his mind that he was once again all alone, but he soon shook his head. That wasn't true. His comrades on this special reconnaissance mission were all still alive. They were simply too absorbed in combat and strayed away from him. If he focused, he could hear Raiden sigh through their linked Para-RAID. He said, with a half-exasperated voice, "Come back already, you moron."

Giving a brief "Yes," Shin turned off the Para-RAID and disembarked from his Juggernaut. The darkening sky lost its vivid blue colors only for a golden sunset to momentarily take its place before melting back into a darker, colder hue of blue. And all around him, as far as he could see, was a crushed and trampled azure that seemed to reflect the heavenly sphere.

Looking back at it, the Juggernaut he had fought in had worn out and damaged its armor and armaments all from the long march and repeated combat all the way here. With this and the armored being clad in the color of dried bone, the whole thing truly looked like a rotting, headless skeleton.

He used Shin's spare parts to replace what had been broken in the battle that started their mission. His high-frequency blade had snapped, its sharp cross section glinting dully in the gloaming. How long had it been since they set out on this special reconnaissance mission? They'd come a long way. They were probably outside the Republic's former territory by now.

Shin narrowed his eyes, recalling the words he entrusted her with. That Handler—Lena—would come to this place.

A cold blue descended on the skies of the Republic capital of Liberté et Égalité, impeded as it was by high-rise buildings. As Lena passed through the garden outside the military HQ on her way home, she suddenly stopped to look up at that lapis lazuli hue.

It was the sky heralding the long autumn night, a dark sky on the cusp of winter, the season of death. *Are Shin and the Spearhead Squadron somewhere out there, under this same sky? Or are they…?*

Where are they now? How far did they go?

Would Lena catch up to them and reach this place where he stands today?

Shin pondered as he watched the sun completely dip into the horizon and a blanket of darkness sink over the field of blue flowers. Would she hold on to that wish until after the war ends? Or would she come here in the middle of the war? The blue flowers of crucifixion bloomed as far as the eye could see. Their vines extended not into the heaven, but crept across the ground, clinging to the soil—bearing their crosses.

He marched, unsure of how far he went, through a battlefield ruled not by men but by the Legion, fighting and pushing forward. Sometimes he couldn't tell if he was still alive or if he'd died. He could feel vividly how many days of endless marching and fighting were gradually whittling him down.

And yet.

Someday, she'll bring flowers.

At his back was his Juggernaut, sprawled out like a bleached corpse, emblazoned with his Personal Mark of a headless skeleton. Even broken, the warrior's skeleton still had a keen edge—like the tip of a sword, like the point of a spear.

And just like that edge, there was one thing that would never fade from his mind, even addled by the battlefield as it was. Her face, unfamiliar though it may be, was the vision he most longed for.

Kitten

Thinking about it reasonably, if there was no room for the Eighty-Six within the eighty-five Sectors, even though they were Republic citizens, surely there would be no room to keep a cat. That strange, dreary thought hung in Lena's mind for a moment as she held up a high-class brand of cat food with a fancy logo on the can.

Since the Republic was surrounded on all fronts by the Legion, the cat food on its store shelves was all synthesized, free of precious rare resources. It looked like meat and smelled like it, too, which meant it was probably better than the synthesized rations the Eighty-Sixth ward got, which the Processors aptly described as "plastic explosives."

Lena wouldn't go so far as to say that one shouldn't own a cat in these conditions, but the fact that the food it got was better than what they sent to other humans could only be described as backward priorities, to put it lightly.

Opening the can with a deep sigh, she poured the oddly stiff glob of synthesized protein—covered in what appeared to be sauce and some other mysterious dressing—onto a plate.

"Here you go. Time to eat."

She knelt and placed the platter in front of a black kitten with white socks sprawled on a cushion in her room's corner. It was the kitten Shin and the Spearhead squadron raised in their barracks. It saw them leave for a battle they would never return from and was left in her care along with their final words. In their eyes, this cat was probably a symbol of a brief, transient time of serenity.

The kitten eyed the needlessly elaborate cat food she placed before it with disinterest, and then looked away. Apparently, the glob of synthesized protein didn't strike it as appetizing. She knew the Spearhead squadron went hunting when they had the chance, so it was probably used to getting scraps of that.

Or maybe...what the kitten didn't like was the fact that Lena took it away to live cooped up inside these walls. Lena's mother insisted that any animal kept by filthy Eighty-Sixers must have been just as dirty, so Lena didn't take the kitten out of her room.

And since she was busy with the new unit she was appointed to, the Brisingamen squadron, she didn't have much time to spend with the kitten during the day. What's more, since the "nature" that decorated the First Sector was all fake, well-prepared, and covered in insecticides and herbicides, there were no bugs or birds outside the window.

Compared to a life where it was free to prowl, where there were animals and bugs to see...and most importantly, where it had a big family in the Spearhead squadron, this life was too different.

"...I'm sorry. You must be lonely with all of them gone."

She softly patted its fluffy fur. The curled-up cat opened one eye and looked up at her emotionlessly. Looking back at him, Lena smiled with a hint of sadness.

"I...I feel lonely, too, without them."

It's been a while since the last five members of the Spearhead squadron left for the eastern front, but she still felt inclined to switch on the Para-RAID at the same time every night. Every night, she would speak with those soldiers whom she only knew by their voices, and every night she looked forward to hearing the composed, serene voice that always greeted her first.

Good evening, Handler One.

Shin. How far have you gone? Where are you right now? Have you fallen? Are you asleep? The fact that I don't even know that...makes me so lonely.

The kitten, who let her pat it to her heart's content so far, stretched out its feet and rubbed its face against her palm. She stood and it nestled against her bosom, letting out a soft meow that was closer to a breath.

I'm lonely. That's what she thought it said.

"Yes."

I'm lonely, without you. I'm terribly lonely.

THE FEDERAL REPUBLIC OF GIAD ARC

They spent their adolescence there, on the battlefield.

EIGHTY-SIX

Life, land, and legacy.
All reduced to a number.

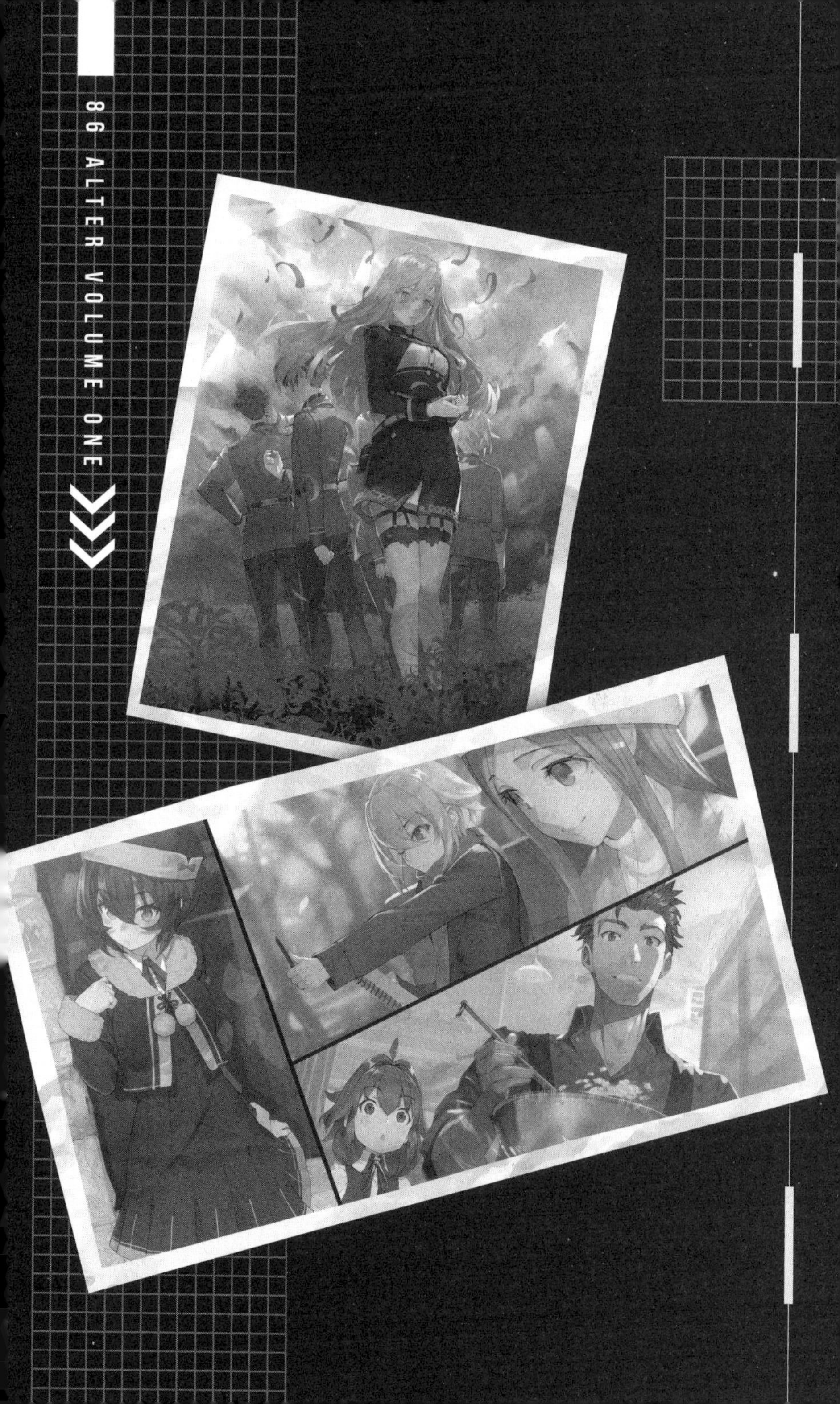
86 ALTER VOLUME ONE

86

EIGHTY-SIX

THE FEDERAL REPUBLIC OF GIAD ARC

Growth

Meals were something Frederica always did on her own. So, having other girls close to her in age there, even if they were older, was a new experience. Her foster father (on paper), Ernst, was always swamped with work and rarely came home, and the maid, Theresa, had her breaks while Frederica dined, so they didn't eat at the same table together. The situation was much the same before she came to this mansion. And so…

"You eat like gluttons, you lot!"

Even if they didn't remember the particular dishes anymore, people remember the cuisine they ate in early childhood for the rest of their lives. Over the last week, Theresa gathered recipes and tried her hand at different kinds of Republic cooking. And so, Frederica now stared with stunned eyes as the dishes on the table were picked clean in moments.

Frederica hadn't finished half her plate yet, unaware she had halted her knife and fork to stare in amazement. Ernst, meanwhile, seemed to have predicted this and called Theresa over with a knowing smile.

Shin, Raiden, and Theo were still in their growth spurts, of course. Kurena and Anju wouldn't grow much taller, but their physiques and figures were still due to settle into feminine maturity. On top of that, years on the battlefield meant that, compared to other boys and girls their age, they had much more muscle mass and a higher metabolism that required more food.

In other words, Ernst had anticipated they would eat this much. Or rather—

"Is there enough, everyone?" Theresa cocked her head, concerned. "I could make second or third servings, if you'd like?"

"Oh… No, it's fine. It was great, though," Raiden said.

"My, I'm glad to hear it. Thank you."

Frederica shuddered, looking upon their exchange. "Wait. Are you to say this is enough to satisfy you…? Just how much can your stomachs contain?"

"You won't grow if you don't eat this much, munchkin," Kurena cooed at Frederica proudly, licking a bit of sauce that stuck to the edge of her lips.

Frederica grumbled, her eyes moving between Kurena, Anju's…and then her own chest, in that order.

Large, appropriately sized, and…relatively restrained (euphemistic language).

"…Is that how it works?" she pondered.

"Hey, what are you looking at, you precocious brat?" Theo asked, impolitely resting his chin on his hand.

"P-precocious brat?! I will have you know I am already nine years of age—old enough to be considered a lady…!"

"Nah, you're a brat."

"Well… I do understand how you feel, but it might be too early for you to start worrying about it."

"Besides, if you start forcing yourself to eat more when you haven't even started growing yet, you'll just end up gaining weight," Shin appended with his usual indifference.

Seeing this, Frederica swung her clenched fists around and stomped her feet in outrage.

"How dare you! The one thing you must not say to a lady's face…!"

"Stop calling yourself a lady, brat."

"Excuse you?!"

Frederica screeched angrily, and the boys kept teasing her like she was a kitten. Ernst watched over this idyllic—if noisy—dinner scene as he tore off a piece of the Federacy's black, heavy bread.

"...It looks like they're doing well enough."

Theresa concurred, with a rare, slight smile on her lips.

Siblings

"Mm. Wait a moment, Shinei."

This department store in central Sankt Jeder was quite bustling, as it was slightly before the Holy Birthday. As they walked through the plaza in front of the store, Frederica said this and stopped in her tracks in front of a small bazaar. Shin, who held her hand because he didn't want to bother looking for her in the crowd, stopped, too.

What drew the small girl's attention was a stall full of handmade toys and handicrafts. Namely, a large stuffed bear toy sitting on display... Or at least, Shin thought it was a bear. For some reason, one of its eyes was stitched on with its seam exposed, and one of its ears had a part missing. It all struck him as somehow very creepy.

"It's still early, but how about picking up a present for the Holy Birthday? I'll cut you a nice price, out of respect for your cute little sister."

A thin, bespectacled woman, seemingly the stall's owner, said this with a bright smile. Frederica wasn't actually related to Shin by blood, but given they both had black hair and bloodred eyes, it was easy to confuse them for siblings.

"B-Big brother, I want it..."

Frederica turned around and took advantage of the situation. She even brought an index finger to her lips and looked at him with upturned eyes.

As Shin wondered where she picked up this particular trick, she realized how embarrassing her actions were and started trembling and going red in the face. Amused, Shin decided to buy her that creepy bear.

Frederica gleefully hugged the bear, which had its price tag clipped off.

"Tee-hee. You're surprisingly gullible, aren't you?"

"Where did you learn to act like that?"

It was surprising, especially considering she was so sheltered she couldn't even go shopping without a chaperone.

"Fool. Surely you don't take me for an impressionable child squealing excitedly at whatever cartoon happens to be on the screen?"

She was very clearly spending hours every day glued to the television and squealing excitedly at cartoons, but Shin kept that comment to himself, knowing that saying it wouldn't do him any good.

"I looked that one up myself," Frederica puffed herself up proudly. "So that when I have to mingle with the common folk, I would draw no suspicion with my..." She then fell silent. "Would not draw attention with my, erm..."

"Conduct?" Shin suggested.

"Aye, indeed... You weren't so mean as to teach me a word that means something else, were you?"

Apparently, she held a grudge after he teased her once.

"I bought you a dictionary. If you don't believe me, you can look it up yourself."

"...Why did you have to buy one made of paper, and the heaviest one imaginable at that...?"

Needless to say, when he went to an antique bookshop, he looked for the largest dictionary he could find with the explicit intent of finding one far too large for Frederica's hands. She initially blustered at him, before becoming incredibly stumped about what to do with the thing. Seeing this, Raiden bought her a pocket-sized dictionary instead, solving that issue.

Hugging the bear so tightly she would have no doubt smothered the thing if it could breathe, Frederica sighed.

"I swear... You can be so childish in the weirdest of ways..."

Shin felt he had no reason to be called that by an actual child. He spotted an old man pass by and glance back at her, seemingly critical of her anachronistic speech patterns.

"If you don't want to draw attention, make a habit of talking like you did back there," he suggested.

Frederica frowned and let out a dissatisfied grumble.

"I would, were I to deem it necessary. But if I were to make speaking as I did earlier a constant, I would look like a buffoon."

"Well, if you don't make a habit of it, you won't know how to do it when it's necessary."

Hearing this made Frederica settle into an odd silence.

"—If you discard the things that make you who you are, can you truly maintain your identity?"

"...?"

"My choice of words is part of what defines me. I cannot discard it as I would a hat, and moreover, I cannot discard who I am."

She spoke softly, burying her chin into the bear's head and her bloodred eyes refusing to look at Shin.

"I don't intend to discard it, and yet... I must conform to the world around me. People can only live among others. So, if you had to choose between conforming and being cast out, which would you pick?"

"..."

He couldn't come up with an answer on the spot. He didn't say anything, but Shin looked down at the back of Frederica's turned head, standing far below him, remembering how they arrived at this topic.

"Is coaxing me into buying you a plush a time when you have to conform?"

This time, it was Frederica who was rendered silent. Seeing her quickly go red in the face, Shin coldly asked a follow-up question.

"And who are you calling 'big brother'?"

"...Silence, silence I say! I hate nothing more than pedantic men."

She thrashed her hands about, but he pushed her small head away. Given the short length of her arms, Frederica's fists failed to reach him, and since she had to hold the plush bear, too, her reach was shorter than usual. She swung the bear at him in an uppercut, but Shin jerked his head away to dodge it.

"...You're going to tear its arm off."

"If that were to happen, I would simply have you sew it back on!

That image alone would make Raiden and the rest of them crack their ribs laughing!"

The girl's loud, shrill voice bellowing at him from so close was cacophonous to his ears. Still pushing Frederica's head away, Shin let out a small sigh.

To those looking on, those two only looked like close siblings messing about. The people walking through the bright town approaching the Holy Birthday looked over at them with a smile.

Shopping

"Raiden, I wish to go shopping."

Frederica was dressed in an adorable outfit—a beret resting on her black hair, an antiquated, lacy red dress, and a fluffy white cat pouch. As she came to him with that demand, Raiden rose from the living room sofa he was lying on. The others were all relaxing nearby…effectively lazing around this afternoon. So, in other words, everyone had free time on their hands.

In the six months or so since they'd come to the capital, they didn't have to fight—which was a good thing—but it did feel like they had a bit too much free time.

"Shopping?"

"Aye. I granted Shinei the honor of escorting me the other day, and today I offer it to you."

Translated from Fredericaese, this meant she had him take her shopping. Her needlessly pretentious way of phrasing it made Shin, who as always had his eyes in a book, crack a thin, sarcastic smile. Seeing him, Raiden let out a tired breath from his nose.

"Well, I guess I've got nothing better to do… What are you shopping for?"

Frederica nodded, all smiles for some reason.

* * *

"I wish to buy a brassier!"

Raiden's mouth fell open. Behind him, Shin let out a strange cough, only just barely stifling a laugh. He then covered his mouth and looked away, trying to keep himself from laughing out loud.

Frederica proudly puffed up her meager chest. "I've recently spotted some signs of growth, and they're quite fearsome if I do say so myself. I'm sure that, come next year, I will be considered a bountiful goddess."

"..."

Sadly, even with her dress thick and meant for winter, her chest looked completely flat.

"No, I think it'll be a while before you need that... But let's drop it for now." Even Raiden, having lived through the cruelty of the Eighty-Sixth Sector's battlefield, wasn't jaded and cold enough to tell her the truth. "How oblivious can you be? You should ask Anju or Kurena for help with that—"

"Oh, you called?"

Anju, who had stepped out earlier, walked back into the room. Raiden made to explain the situation, but before he could, Shin cut into his words.

"Anju, do you need to go shopping? I'll carry your bags."

"Huh? I'd appreciate it, but why this, all of a sudden?"

"Don't worry about it." Shin gently pushed her back, ushering her out into the corridor.

Too embarrassed to speak up, Kurena missed her chance to ask to come along, so Theo took her hand and led her out of the room, too.

"I'll go with Kurena, then. But you know, Kurena, you should have asked to tag along right away back there. Stuff like this is why he always sees you as a kid sister."

"Wh-what? No! It's not like that!"

"Yeah, yeah. Shiiin, how about we catch a movie while we're at it, the four of us? There's that one film, right? I don't remember what it's called. The one that looked boring."

"You mean that weird documentary? Sure, let's do it. Looks dull, though."

"...Why go watch a movie if you know it's boring?" Anju asked suspiciously. "Plus, what about Raiden and Frederica...?"

Shrugging off her question, the four of them walked off, their voices growing distant. Raiden, who watched this all play out in dumbfounded silence, finally came to. Standing in front of him was Frederica, who was clearly very adamant about going shopping, her eyes alight with hopes and expectations for a bountiful future. Raiden could hear, from the front door down the hall, the sound of a lock turning and hinges screeching.

"Hey, Shin! Wait up!"

Followed by the sound of the door cruelly closing.

Five minutes later, Anju got Shin to spill the beans and hurried back home, saving Raiden from catastrophe.

Within Walking Distance

Thankfully, Shin and the other four got used to life in Sankt Jeder faster than expected. Ernst pondered this as he flipped through a newspaper, glancing over to the lively living room that had more than doubled its population.

Still, the five had spent too long in the internment camps and battlefield—far too long isolated from modern life. And that had made them feel a little... No, very off-kilter here.

"Ah, the moron finally picked up... Hey, Shin! Where are you?! You're past curfew!"

"Raiden, you're like his mom," Kurena remarked, holding back a chuckle.

"...What are you, my mom?" Shin's voice said roughly the same thing at the same time through the phone's speaker.

They were in the mansion's living room right before dinner. Ernst set them a relatively early curfew to get them used to having a leisurely dinner again. Shin was late, then, while the other four were home. Theresa was in the kitchen, concerned while making dinner, as Frederica was seated on one side of the sofa, cranky over an empty stomach, squeezing the plush bear Shin bought her the other day with a hug.

Raiden snarled at him to pipe down and asked.

"Where are you right now?"

"The war memorial."

...What did he go there for?

Ernst put down the newspaper, baffled, as the boys' conversation continued.

"And that's why you turned off your phone."

It was only respectful to turn off your phone in a memorial that also served as a museum, after all.

"Yeah. I found some interesting records in the library, and related documents were on display at the war memorial. I know the librarian, and she told me it wasn't far, so I figured I'd go and take a look."

The library Shin was talking about was likely the central capital library at the city center, while the war memorial was in the capital outskirts. There was a bus line connecting the two, though, so they weren't far, relatively speaking.

"I decided to look at the other exhibits, too, and ended up talking to some old man."

The old man had asked Shin if he was a student, telling him he was impressed that a boy his age would come here on a day off. He said he had actually participated in a battle Shin was looking up. The man kept regaling him with his martial stories, and the hours passed by. They ended up moving to a café in the hall, and the old man treated him to coffee and cookies, and, for some reason, the curators joined in on their conversation, too, listening to his tales.

"...You could have found a polite way to leave, you know," Raiden said, looking fed up.

"No, his story was pretty interesting. He was on the front lines the whole time until he was discharged, so there was plenty to learn. And

it was pretty fun how the number of enemies he took down got bigger every time he mentioned it."

Eventually, the café owner got tired of waiting for them to finish and gently urged the old man to go back to his wife, Shin to go back to his family, and the curators to go back to work.

"And you stayed out this late."

"Sorry… I'll get back as soon as I can. And I'm sorry to ask you for this after I'm late, but let Theresa know."

They could hear the faint sound of footsteps over snow-covered flagstones. He was out of the war memorial and walking with the swift, rhythmic steps of a soldier, like a march. Still, as Ernst thought it would take him an hour to get back by bus, Shin spoke over the phone.

"It'll take me three hours. It's snowing, so it'll take me a while to get back to the city center."

"Oh… Yeah, it'll take that long by foot. Got it. We'll go ahead and eat, then. Frederica's all moody, because she's hungry."

"No, hold on a moment!" Ernst called out, drawing dubious stares from the five children. He couldn't see Shin over the phone, but he probably had much the same expression. Ernst talked on, undisturbed.

"There's a bus stop next to the memorial hall! Take a bus! They come every fifteen minutes at this hour!"

There was a pause.

"Finding it is a drag."

"How is spending a few minutes looking for the bus stop a drag when walking for three hours isn't?! If you can't find it, go back to the memorial and ask the staff! You'll find it if you go back, it's right in front of the place!"

Shin sounded incredibly reluctant, but he could hear him turn around. The sound of the snow crunching under his steps stopped for a moment, and then resumed.

"Shin, don't tell me you walked all the way from the library to the memorial…?"

"That's what I did."

"When there were buses driving past you the whole way?! Didn't you consider taking one? I told you when you first came here that capital citizens can take the bus for free, remember?!"

"...Yeah."

Apparently, none of that occurred to him, and he forgot.

"I just figured I'd stretch my legs, and this counted as a bit of a long walk."

"That's more than just a walk! No one calls walking three hours by foot a stroll!"

Yes, having spent so long riding those defective Feldreß called Juggernaut, they were used to their only movement options being either by Juggernaut or by foot. And since they lost their Juggernauts in the Legion's territories, their only remaining movement option was going by foot. They had no idea about public transportation, like buses and trains, to begin with.

And so, after a long life of walking everywhere on foot, they were much more used to walking than the average Federacy citizen and had a much wider idea of what counts as being "within walking distance." When they first came to Sankt Jeder, Ernst's secretary escorted Anju when she went out on "a little walk," only to end up following her to Sankt Jeder's outskirts and climbing up a small mountain. By the end of it, Anju was looking down on his secretary (a twenty-five-year-old male) who was exhausted at the peak and gasping for air, his hands on his knees.

Ernst wasn't going to complain about them having good stamina. Walking made for good exercise and kept them healthy. But them saying a three-hour walk was "within walking distance" was clearly abnormal.

"If it's just one station away, walking there is fine, but past that, use public transportation! Or at least ride a bicycle!"

In fact, Raiden had a part-time job delivering packages with his bike, so Ernst would have expected him, out of all five of them, to be the first to point out that going this far on foot was strange.

But sadly, despite his expectations, Raiden was looking at him dubiously.

"But going all the way to the stop would just—"

"I keep telling you! Going to the station and catching a bus would save you time! Oh, enough!"

Frederica listened in on their exchange with her mouth hanging open while Theresa picked up the shards of a plate she dropped in the kitchen (Theo noticed and went to get a broom to help her). Ernst cradled his head, exasperated.

The people of the Republic really did some serious damage to these kids, didn't they?

"Once we restore relations with them, can I smack the Republic's president or something for this?!"

To think they threw even their most basic values off-kilter!

Patrol Duty

The body armor he wore over his field uniform was only good for blocking small shell fragments at best. It was powerless when it came to blocking more destructive rifle rounds. The shield and the weapon have waged war for a long time over which was superior at protecting the fragile human body, but in modern warfare, the weapon emerged as the clear victor. Especially when this weapon—when firearms—were being wielded by an opponent that wasn't human.

"Run, run, run! The moment you stop running, you die, brats!"

Spurred on by the drill sergeant's shouting, young men and women ran through the faded concrete walls of the abandoned city ruins with expressions of effort and fear. Urban camouflage field uniforms were no longer in use by the Federacy military, but the special officer cadets were given these old hand-me-down uniforms out of budget concerns.

They weren't equipped with the armored skeleton that became the standard issue of Federacy military infantry, but old-fashioned rifles, and were sent out to the battlefield on patrol practice to build up their courage.

There was no Legion conflict in this area yet—it *should have* been safe.

But they crept through the shadows of the ruins, drawing close to their targets by sliding across the ground with the sound of bones rustling, a sound far too faint to match their incredible weight.

The composite sensors on their torsos turned to look at the cadets' fleeing backs, and their two anti-personnel machine guns revolved and spewed out sweeping gunfire. Their powerful 7.62 mm rounds easily penetrated the cadets' body armor, freely tumbling inside their bodies and unleashing their kinetic energy into their brittle human flesh.

"Whoa, ah, aaah…!"

As pieces of concrete ricocheted off the ground around him, Eugene stumbled out of the Ameise's firing zone. Calling the way he desperately fled its sweeping fire "clumsy" would be a generous way of putting it, but he was in no condition to care about appearances.

"This way, Eugene."

Apparently, there were Legion deployed all over the city ruins. The deafening roaring of machine-gun fire and the sound of assault rifle rounds were audible from every direction, along with angry shouting and screaming. And, despite that, the voice seemed to penetrate all that noise in its silent serenity. Eugene turned to look in a daze, spotting a slender figure clad in the same uniform as him, motioning for him to come over from the shadow of the rubble.

The others were boys around his age, dressed in the same dusty field uniforms and helmets and with similar physiques, so Eugene had a hard time telling his fellow cadets apart. But for some reason, this guy he could recognize—by the cold, penetrating bloodred eyes peering at him through his dust-proof goggles.

"…Shin!"

"Hurry. The Ameise are coming."

At Shin's urging, Eugene dived into the cover of the rubble, with Shin grabbing him by the arm and pulling him in. The next moment, Ameise machine-gun fire swept across the spot he had occupied seconds ago.

Seeing bullets whiz through the street he had just been running down and the spot he had been standing froze the blood in Eugene's veins. Shin, by contrast, calmly replaced his assault rifle's depleted magazine. Eugene didn't know how, but he was terribly calm even in this hectic situation. He looked up at the sky with all the indifference of a man checking for rain.

"I was thinking they deployed faster than their usual movement speed. So that's why."

There were Ameise and anti-personnel self-propelled mines *raining down* on them. The Ameise had their six legs spread out while the self-propelled mines were on all fours. With their parachutes open, they drifted away from the blue sky and landed with a rumble, kicking up dust, and began their silent creep forward, their footsteps as quiet as the Legion's movement always was.

"I guess it makes sense. Cannons have been firing ten-tonne shells dozens of kilometers away for a long time now, so it's possible, if reckless. Or maybe they loaded units into missiles and had them descend from midair… Though it'd make for a pretty absurd image if a steam or electromagnetic catapult did it."

Shin sighed. Eugene couldn't help but cut into his words.

"Shin! Stop it! This isn't the time to analyze what they're doing!"

"No, this is actually good news, as these things go. If they deployed the way I think they did, they shouldn't be able to propel any Grauwolf or Löwe. If it's just self-propelled mines and Ameise, we can weather an assault this size."

As he spoke, his bloodred eyes looked ahead. He aimed his assault rifle and squeezed the trigger, the bullet hitting the center mass of a humanoid figure trying to sneak up on them from behind the rubble. It fell to the ground, and for a moment Eugene saw its head, a sphere lacking any eyes, mouth, or nose—a self-propelled mine.

Shin only fired a single round while their fellow cadets were trying to fight off the Legion with their guns blaring at full auto. Judging that even firing a short burst would be excessive against a weak self-propelled mine—and while using a bulky, hard-to-handle 7.62 assault rifle with considerable recoil—he accurately shot it down with one round.

"…We can handle these numbers so long as we coordinate with the others, but it doesn't look like anyone here's good enough to fight, and I think pushing it would just get people killed. That's not worth it in this situation."

He said this calmly. Eugene looked at him, stunned.

"...Uh, Shin."

"What?"

"Why...are you so used to this?"

To the battlefield. To fighting an enemy as vast and undefeatable for a flesh and blood human as the Legion. Shin was a cadet just like Eugene, right? A fresh cadet on the battlefield for the first time... Right?

Shin looked at Eugene with indifference and shrugged once.

"I'll tell you when we get back."

He said this, clearly assuming they would get back from what felt to Eugene like a battle where they were teetering on the jagged edge of life and death. And Shin assumed that it was like nothing at all—calmly, like, all of this just came naturally to him.

Like a battle-hardened warrior, used to standing on the razor's edge. Like the grim reaper.

What Hides Behind the Monster's Mask

In the end, only a dozen or so members, herself included, survived the major operation to destroy the Morpho. The commander of the artillery unit, with her glasses' lenses cracked and their black rims bent, walked with an air of shame through the noise as the bridgehead for the Republic's rescue was being set up.

She spotted a familiar face in one part of the camp and approached him.

"You're from artillery. Looks like you made it, too."

"Yeah, *at least I did.*"

His tone made her stop in her tracks. She could tell even without looking, but the commander of his unit's accompanying infantry unit, who'd often exchange jabs with him after missions, was nowhere to be seen.

The young artillery commander looked ahead with a look in his eye he never showed before, and jerked his chin with an expression he never showed before.

"If *they* were fine…I was going to blame them for not taking that monster down faster."

It happened shortly before that.

"…Mm?"

As he walked through the block assigned to the Nordlicht squadron, he spotted Fido's hulking form crouching in one corner and stopped in his tracks. Or rather, he spotted the slender shape leaning against Fido's body.

Shin was leaning against its sooty frame, warm from the autumn sun, with Fido offering him shade. He was asleep.

Seriously, this guy…

Raiden dropped his shoulders. After the operation was over, Shin talked to them via the Para-RAID. Raiden didn't know what happened, but the dangerous air that hung over Shin had finally slipped away. He wasn't sure why, but maybe Shin came to terms with things in his own way. And he was probably tired… All the fatigue from days of consecutive activity and his nerves being on edge from continued combat finally got the better of him, and he fell asleep.

Shin probably intended to just shut his eyes for a bit, but seeing him sleep out in the afternoon sun, all defenseless—albeit in the middle of their army's camp—made Raiden sigh.

…Raiden couldn't deny being tired, and the weather really was nice. Plus, everyone in the squad, Raiden included, had their Juggernauts busted and had effectively nothing to do. All in all, getting some rest when you can is part of being prepared for battle.

"Fido, I'll be taking the corner, okay?"

"*Pi.*"

"Ah, Fido, me too, me too!"

* * *

"Oh, everyone's taking a nap? Let me join in too, Fido."

"Maybe I should lie down, too… Fido, can you fit me over there?"

"…Oh?"

As she watched the maintenance team quite literally swoop over to repair the Juggernauts, Grethe spotted a small figure pass her by. Frederica was laboriously carrying several blankets provided by the military in her small arms.

"Why are you carrying those around?"

"Oh, Grethe! I am relieved to see you are safe… Oh, this."

The bundle of blankets were relatively heavy. With her feeble arms trembling, Frederica shrugged proudly and with a hint of relief.

"My older brothers and sisters are a troublesome lot, is all. Do not worry about it, I needn't your help with this."

The artillery captain looked in the direction indicated by the armored unit commander, and was rendered speechless. Lying nestled together in the shadow of some unfamiliar type of what looked like a transport drone, were five boys and girls in their teens.

They were likely exhausted, as all the noise around them did nothing to wake them up. Apparently, someone looked after them, because blankets were draped over them all, if a bit crookedly. And, on closer inspection, there was a sixth person sleeping there. A young girl—a Mascot, from the looks of it—was curled up and sleeping in the blanket of the black-haired boy in the center of the group.

These child soldiers, still young enough to be considered kids, were they the ones forced to shoulder the fate of the Federacy, of all mankind…?

"I kept hearing that they were brats…and what do you know, they really are."

They were not the monsters of the Republic. The artillery unit commander trembled, hanging his head in an attempt to suppress an emotion surging up in him.

"Dammit. I can't say anything to their faces...!"

Because he just understood that calling this "barking up the wrong tree" would be an understatement...

The sleeping children didn't react, of course, but the drone turned its round optical sensors at them and let out a small electronic "*Pi.*" It serenely looked at anyone who approached, like a large dog guarding the master that nestled against it.

Looking back at it, the artillery captain spoke up.

"Let's go. They're the biggest contributors to this operation, and we can't disturb their rest. But next time... Next time, we'll tell them we don't need their help; that we're the ones who put in the effort to get this far, and we'll keep on doing so."

"...Yeah." The artillery unit commander smiled faintly, but she was still hanging her head. "You're right. Next time, we'll show these kids... we can get by without having to rely on brats to fight our battles for us."

The Reaper Meets a Doting Big Brother & a Straitlaced Relative

As the turning of the seasons was dipping into winter, the flowers blooming all around were golden springtime rape flowers. Despite the battle taking place in abandoned city ruins, that spot alone was an open field with nothing to obscure the blue sky.

Sitting at the center of the field and brusquely disturbing the overly pastoral scenery were two steel-gray shadows.

"...What's wrong, Shin? You look pale."

One stood 4 m tall. Its massive weight alone served as a lethal weapon, and it was equipped with an imposing 155 mm tank turret. It was a Dinosauria, with Liquid Micromachine hands sprouting out of it.

"Did you fall ill, Shinei? Looking after your health is a warrior's duty. I know you just fought me, but you're letting your focus slip too much. Don't besmirch the Nouzen name."

The second one was even larger, standing 11 meters tall and 40 meters long with an 800 mm railgun. The Morpho spoke.

What the hell?

As Shin asked himself this, the two Legion continued with the serene, calm conversation that didn't match their monstrous appearances. A small white butterfly fluttered between the human and two machines.

"I haven't had this talk with Shin, now that you mention it. Eighty percent of the time he's just gushing about Dad and Mom."

"You absolutely should have had that talk with him… He lost his mother and father. If he were to be ignorant of his lineage on top of that he'd lose one of the things that make him who he is."

"True. So…"

The Dinosauria turned to look at him (probably?), intending to say something, but Shin cut him off.

"Brother."

"Mm?"

"Could you at least show the way you looked when you were alive?"

"That's a bit of a tall order… Plus, this is what I looked like when I was alive, in a sense."

The idea of a copy of his brain extracted at the brink of death counting as "alive" was one that didn't sit well with Shin.

"And you're already older than I was when you're supposed to be four years younger than me. It's an outrage."

That's not my problem.

"It makes it hard to talk to you, and it makes my neck hurt. I don't know where I'm supposed to look. Besides, you're both completely dead, so don't show up anymore."

"But I'm worried about my cute kid brother—"

"Don't. Show up. Anymore."

Hearing Shin say this flatly, Rei let out a deep sigh.

"You know, there was a time when you always ran after me, calling my name. Now all that angelic innocence is gone."

"Who do you think made that happen?"

Having been hit by that megatonne punch of a retort, Rei hung his head dejectedly (his turret and frame tilted to their lowest angle of elevation). Kiriya, meanwhile, let out an exasperated sigh…or so Shin thought. The massive spear-like blades that made up the Morpho's turret shook up and down, whooshing through the air.

"Well… I suppose I can understand fretting over your younger brother, but…"

"Right? My younger brother's adorable. You can't have him, though."

"I don't want him. And I never said that, either. I'll be honest, he's anything but charming."

"I dunno about that… He's a bit aloof, but that's just what boys his age are like. I think it's cute enough. And you're a lot like that yourself, Kiriya. You try really hard to make yourself look cool."

"…I should have blasted you, too, while I was doing that test fire…"

"Aha-ha, you couldn't have. I outranked you, as commanding units go."

"Tsk…"

A Dinosauria gushing over his kid brother, and a Morpho acting annoyed at that display of affection. It was a sight that took a toll on Shin's spirits, and honestly, just having to look at them made him tired. It didn't take long for a fed up Shin to speak.

"…Brother."

"Mm? What's wrong, Shin?"

"Can I wake up now?"

"Oh, sure. Good luck today."

"Look after the princess. Don't let anyone harm a single hair on her head."

Only when the scenery was beginning to fade did he see two figures—one in a desert camouflage field uniform and the other in black-and-red uniform—wave, and it honestly annoyed him to no end.

* * *

When he opened his eyes, he found himself peering up at the artificial-looking ceiling of the barracks' shelter module. It was a portable, collapsible living space, easy to transport in large numbers via truck, and only required a few soldiers to set up.

Raiden—who stayed in the same room as Shin, since they were in the same Republic relief unit—peered at him.

"...You were turning in your sleep, man."

"Yeah, that makes sense." Shin sat up in his pipe bed, holding his head, which ached even though he hadn't overslept.

Seriously. If they didn't have to show up absurdly like that...he'd have a lot to say to them. Especially his brother.

The Low-Flying Great Bird

It came as little surprise that the Nachzehrer was completely trashed after the operation.

"...Grethe is over the moon for a chance to make a second one, it seems."

Upon returning to the 177th division base, they found the shutter at the back of the hangar wide open, permanently vacated of its occupant. Gazing at the empty blackness of the room, Frederica said this, and Shin held his tongue for a moment. Their lieutenant colonel was by no means a bad person, but...

"Even if we could fly it again, there's no use for it anymore..."

The requirements to get it to work were too costly for it to be practical. And frankly, the thing wasn't made for land combat.

"I doubt anyone would say it's worth the budget it would take to make it anymore. There aren't any facilities to produce one, either."

"Its name is too ominous as it is. A vampire creeping about, dragging its shadow along... 'Tis the name of the dead. Far too ominous for a battlefield where we must stand on the edge of life and death."

"..."

If this was the logic she was going with, Reginleif was the name of a Valkyrie gathering the souls of dead soldiers from the battlefield to recruit them into the god of war's army. Vánagandrs were named after another name for the world-destroying giant wolf. The Úlfhéðnar Armored Skeletons were named after berserker warriors.

The entirety of the Federacy's naming scheme when it came to weapons was questionable, given that they were used defensively. They weren't much different from the Republic, who named their weapon a Juggernaut, after a deformed god who trampled people in the name of salvation.

"It had another name during prototype stage, though."

When they got back to base, Shin had the head of maintenance show him the Nachzehrer old documentation. It was planned and sold to the military by the president of WHM–Wenzel und Heinrich Motors—then a warplane maker. Said president was Grethe's father… Apparently his daughter took after him, in ways both good and bad.

"Oh? What was it?"

"Yohanoyataniyakumonomimatori."

"T-Taniyakumonomima…?"

"Yohanoyataniyakumonomimatori."

"Yohano…yata… It's unspeakable! What is this ridiculous name?!"

"That's why it didn't work as a warplane's name. Too much of a tongue twister."

Even if it would be called using a callsign during combat.

"Then how didn't you bite your tongue trying to say it?!"

"I'm honestly not sure about that myself."

Given that it was a word from another language type, he couldn't even tell where one word ended and another started.

"Apparently, it's a great bird from some far eastern myth or story, perfect for a bird that swoops through the air by creeping over the ground, but it was too obscure, and the name got turned down."

"Whoever named it wears their influences on their sleeve a bit too proudly… 'Tis the mixing of business with personal taste…," Frederica grumbled with a face of disgust. Shin shrugged indifferently.

It was difficult to read on top of being hard to pronounce, but there was another reason the great bird's name was rejected in the development phase.

"They also turned it down because they knew that if this was its official name, people would tease the Mascots by getting them to fumble saying it."

"...?! Is that not precisely what you just did with me?! Did you do that on purpose?!"

He did, of course.

Frederica noticed that he'd been trying to hold back laughter. Looking down at her angrily glinting bloodred eyes, much like his own, Shin said, "Try it one more time, for me."

"Yohanonyataniyakumonimimatori! There, satisfied, you ingrate?!"

Frederica defiantly bellowed at him, stumbling and slurring the name, at which point Shin couldn't keep himself from laughing out loud.

Incidentally, the Nachzehrer Mk. II's budget was unanimously rejected. On top of its low-cost effectiveness, the Mk.II's "new proposed features of fusion and transformation" and "the super high caliber cannon to be placed at the plane's nose" were cited as the key reasons for the rejection.

Prank (Lena → Shin)

After knocking on the door to the common room open to both men and women, Lena opened it and found Shin asleep on the bench at the back of the room. She blinked, taken aback by this uncommon sight. This was the locker room for the Processors in Rüstkammer base, the home base for the Eighty-Sixth Strike Package. He had his arms folded—perhaps out of habit—with his back against the wall as he slept quietly.

Lena grinned, her eyes still wide from surprise. Their all-night combat exercise at the maneuvering ground at the back of the base had concluded, and they just finished their debriefing. She noticed she hadn't seen Shin since and wondered where he'd gone off to.

During last night's training drill, Shin's unit—being the most senior one—served as the aggressor in the exercise. But even they, who had the most combat experience of all surviving Processors, were tired after such prolonged activity.

They had spoken for six months two years ago, but this was her first time actually seeing Shin asleep. After all, they had been talking via Para-RAID, which required both parties to be conscious to work, meaning Shin couldn't resonate to begin with while sleeping.

Lena approached him, giddy at this new experience. She kept the sounds of her pumps clicking against the floor as quiet as possible, so as to not rouse him from his rest. She leaned in, peering closely at his sleeping face as he hung his neck.

Given his taciturn personality, Shin occasionally wore a very cool-headed expression, but his sleeping face now had no hint of coldness, making him look surprisingly young. Maybe he just looked his age… But this just showed how on edge he usually was. This boy in his late teens, same as her, had to be more tense than a boy his age should ever be.

This made her consider if she should wake him up and tell him to go to his room—as they were given the day after the exercise off—but seeing him so sound asleep made her think twice about waking him.

Spurred by a part of her that didn't want him to wake quite yet, Lena continued quietly, wordlessly observing how he slept. It was like she was looking at some untamed animal of the wilderness sleep for the first time. She'd be much too embarrassed to dare look at him at this proximity while he was awake, so this was her first chance to look at him up close.

His face had the smooth, graceful facial features typical of former Imperial nobility. If she didn't know better, and if he wasn't still in his panzer jacket after the exercise, she wouldn't think he's a soldier at all.

And, ah, his lashes are long.

That thought spurred her to reach out without even realizing it. For his gentle eyelids, now closed, were adored with lashes a different color from hers. To the faint scar lingering on his forehead above his left eye. To the line of his cheeks, in the height of transitioning from the gentleness of a boy to the more virile, pronounced shape of a man.

What would it feel like…if she touched them?

But then, suddenly, the door to the shower on the other side of the locker room opened with a loud clatter.

"Ah, now I feel better! Uh…"

Shiden stepped out boisterously, her red hair still dripping with water and her sinewy limbs obscured by her flight suit and a tank top—noticeably without any underwear.

"Oh, Your Majesty. Yer pullin' a prank on him? Want me to step out?"

Lena stumbled in quick steps, red in the face, skittering back to the locker room entrance in the blink of an eye.

"N-no! I wasn't thinking of doing anything like pinching his nose or squishing his cheeks!"

"…No, uh, when I said prank, I didn't mean the childish sort…"

"E-erm, I, uh, it's a nice day out so I need to go comb my plant's data terminal, and uh, I need to finish configuring my potted cat! So, bye!"

Stammering this incoherent excuse, the Bloodstained Queen—now red up to her ears—bolted out of the locker room. She was so disoriented that she tripped over herself three times and disappeared into the corridor, with the sound of her clicking pumps trailing loudly behind her.

Seeing her off, Shiden turned her eyes back to the locker room.

"Now, then. I know yer awake, Casanova," she said, her odd-eyed gaze fixed on Shin, who opened his own bloodred eyes. "How long were ya awake?"

"I'd wake up even if I didn't want to, what with you two screeching right in front of me."

Apparently, he was pretending to be asleep, having come to the instinctual conclusion that opening his eyes would just further complicate the situation.

"Mmmmmmm." Shiden, on the other hand, smirked at him.

"…What?" Shin's expression contorted in displeasure.

"Oh, nothin', really. I was just thinkin' that if it were me sneakin' up on you like that, you'd have woken up much sooner."

"..."

He seemed to have noticed the teasing air to her voice. Shin squinted at her in displeasure, but Shiden paid it no mind and smirked.

"And I'm better than her at masking my presence, too. Her Majesty can't mask her presence at all, actually... Ya really let down yer guard around her, don'cha? Imagine that. The Li'l Reaper from the eastern front."

Prank (Shin → Lena)

Annette looked up to the sound of the lab door sliding open, her expression turning puzzled upon spotting Lena there.

"...What happened to your hair?"

"Erm... I honestly don't know myself...," Lena said, cocking her head.

The tuft of her head that she'd dyed crimson, the one hanging on the side of her face, was braided despite her not remembering having done this.

"It was like this when I woke up, for some reason."

It happened some time earlier. Lena wasn't used to working with electronic documents, leading to her work dragging out. As a result, she hadn't slept in days. Seeing this, Shin came to her office's attached lounge to help her work.

Hearing Lena rise from her desk, Shin looked up. He'd told her to get some sleep earlier, but his tactical commander remained attached to her desk from sheer guilt. Now, however, her eyelids were clearly falling, her back—usually held straight—was slumped, and she was wobbling on her feet.

This went beyond being sleepy; at this point she looked less alive than a zombie in a horror movie. It was very strange. A bit overwhelmed by how she seemed to have broken some kind of limit and reached the point where her reasoning had snapped, Shin called out to her.

"...Lena?"

"Shin... Could you...please lend me your back for a bit...?"

...Huh?

Before that puzzling thought could register in his mind, he felt a lightweight lean against his uniformed back. Staying still, he moved his eyes, spotting Lena, seated on the sofa and already fast asleep with her small head leaning just under his shoulder.

He could feel her body heat, lower than his own, and her shallow breathing. A whiff of her perfume filled his senses. It all coalesced into one, freezing his thoughts.

Erm. I guess this is fine?

He was used to staying still during ambushes. Letting go of his thoughts for a split second, Shin allowed himself to enjoy the situation. Or rather, he tried, but his share of the work was unfinished. And once he was done with that, he'd effectively be left with nothing to do. His bloodred eyes stared up into the air and suddenly they settled on something silver.

As she opened the heavy door to the commander's office with some effort, she happened upon that sight. Frederica stood rooted in place out of sheer confusion.

"Shinei... What are you doing?"

"I'm bored."

"No... I, erm, I can see that..."

Lena was leaning against him, her cheek smushed against his back as she slept, which meant he couldn't move. Which was...understandable, if not exactly acceptable. But what she really wanted to comment on was that Shin was holding one strand of silvery hair hanging over his shoulder and continually braiding it.

Since Shin's hair was short, surely he never learned how to braid on his own (Most boys didn't, with some exceptions like Kiriya, who combed her hair every morning and whom she asked to tie it up in some simple ways; Raiden, who seemed to be good with his hands in general; and Theo, who had tried out some complex hairstyle for her the last time she asked). He was going about it slowly and with clearly unpracticed fingers, but he braided her silvery locks all the way to their end, then undid the braid and started over.

He did so like he was enjoying the feel of her soft, well-kept hair. Lovingly, even… Even though touching one's hair was said to be a deeper expression of affection than sharing one's bed.

"…You look quite happy."

"Yeah," he admitted it instantly, probably without realizing it.

Frederica let out an exasperated sigh. "…If you cannot move, I shall beckon Anju over to help. Wait a minute."

"Mm…?"

Lena herself didn't remember what she had been doing before she fell asleep. As she kept cocking her head quizzically, Annette frowned. Either way…

"Are you going to unbraid that thing?"

The braid was terribly done, and Annette had to ask. It wasn't even properly trisected and was both twisted and kinked. Whoever did it forgot the order of how to braid them halfway through, and the stitches were uneven at points… They were either very clumsy or extremely inexperienced at it.

Overall, it looked like the kind of unsightly, poorly made braid a child would make.

"I should, but…," Lena said, picking up the tuft of her hair that was tied into a braid.

The unpracticed, childish way it was braided came across as a bit confused…but also, loving.

"…It feels like a waste."

Her Majesty Works Out

A jersey and T-shirt that made for a mix of Prussian blue and snow white; brand-new, sparkling sneakers; a pair of shorts that really accentuated her pale, untanned thighs. She had a towel with a print of the Strike Package's *86* symbol—courtesy of the base's PX—draped over her neck and a cloth bib with her name, *Lena*, printed onto it with big letters emblazoned over her shirt's chest.

"...Lena, what is this outfit you're wearing?"

They were in the Strike Package's home base's—Rüstkammer's—maneuvering grounds. Shin blinked upon spotting his tactical commander dressed in unusual attire. He was in the Federacy's combat fatigues after a personal training session.

Lena answered, excited at wearing a different outfit than usual as girls often are, "It's a gym uniform!"

"Yes, I can see that. What I mean is, the kind of personal training combatants do might be a bit too hard for you."

The umbrella term "uniform" covers quite a few sets of clothes, from dress uniforms for formal occasions, to work uniforms used every day, and combat fatigues used during operations and training. But, as the Republic military had no "human" combatants, it had all but abolished combat fatigues.

Shin recognized this was a gym uniform, but as their commander, Lena's stamina and physique was different from his and the Processors'. She wouldn't just be unable to keep up with their training, it could outright be damaging to her body.

"Don't worry, I have my own personal training menu set up."

"Well, that's fine, so long as you're careful... But why are you working out?"

Shin had no objection to her building up her stamina, but it wasn't like being out of shape impeded her performance as a commander. Lena's eyes, however, reacted to his question with a bit of a flustered expression.

"Erm... Well, you see..."

Her argent eyes darted about in embarrassment... But upon seeing Shin narrow his eyes at her dubiously, she worked up the courage to say it.

"I actually...got a little fat!"

...*You did?* Shin asked himself.

Having grown up on the battlefield, they all had very developed muscles, even the girls. Since Shin was used to everyone around him being relatively bulked up, Lena actually struck him as thin and slender. So much so he had to wonder if she was eating enough.

Lens pumped her fists up and down as she fervently explained, ignorant of Shin's thoughts.

"All the food's been so tasty since I came to the Federacy! The meat, bread, and vegetables are all real...!"

Unlike the Republic, which relied almost entirely on the synthesized food from production plants, the Federacy had fresh produce, which was preferentially circulated to the army.

"Mealtimes are always so much fun, so you see, I just end up overeating, and..."

"Yesterday's *eisbein* and simmered sausages were tasty," Shin noted.

"They were. The meat was really thick and the sauerkraut and mustard added that extra sour flavor... Wait, no!" Lena nodded, getting carried away, but then snapped out of it and drew closer to him. She was teary-eyed for some reason. "I mean, when it comes to girls, you prefer... you know, thin, slender girls, right?!"

"No, I, erm..." Shin nearly blurted out an answer but managed to catch himself at the last second. That was close.

Lena realized that she made a pretty careless remark, too, and the two fell silent for a second.

"So, yes, I'm exercising and going on a diet! Come summer, I'll be a new me!"

Why summer?

The fires of war had burned away much of his memories of

peacetime, so Shin forgot the one event that was something of a staple of summertime.

"There's nothing wrong with staying in shape, if you ask me...but just don't overdo it. It'll all be for nothing if you end up hurting your body in the process."

"Ah... Yes, you're right. Thank you..."

"By the way, we're having veal schnitzel for lunch today. Try not to eat too much this time."

"...Bully! Jerk!" Lena puffed up her cheeks in a pout and took off to the maneuvering ground by herself...as Shin sat down, planning to step in if he saw her embark on an exercise she wasn't used to.

HELP! (Lena's POV)

Typically, men are stronger than women.

Lena knew this, but she didn't imagine it'd be that hard to shake off a man's strength, or that she'd be completely immobile if one held her in his embrace.

So it was that Lena ended up unable to move, with her and Shin lying on their sides on a cramped bed. His arms, wrapped over her body and curled over her back, were solid, muscular, and incredibly heavy. Their combined body heats were suffocatingly hot. Especially her face. Why does she feel like she's on fire?

There was faint breathing over her head, but she could hardly hear it over the loud thumping of her heart in her ears.

Annette peered into the room through the entrance, and then asked with an expression that was part amazement and part annoyance, "...What are you doing, Lena?"

"Help me."

"Thanks for the treat, I guess."

What?!

"Or did I come here after you got made into a treat? Should I get the party confetti?"

"No! Listen, what happened was—"

* * *

It was some thirty minutes ago. As Lena walked down the hall of the base where they were stationed in Liberté et Égalité, she ran into Shin, wobbling unsteadily down an empty corridor in neither their assigned office block nor the Processors' residential block.

Following the increase of the intelligent Legion during the recapture of Charité underground terminal, Shin was under the weather for a few days. He couldn't stay awake and spent entire days asleep. Seeing as he was out of bed, he was probably feeling better that day, but on closer inspection, his eyes were barely half-open. He was unsteady on his feet, too, and the towel he was wearing over his tank top was sliding off, like he was a small child.

In other words, he was half asleep.

"Shin."

Only when she called his name did it seem to register for Shin that Lena was standing right in front of him.

"...Lena."

"What are you doing out here?"

"Nothing... I figured I'd take a shower to keep myself awake, but for some reason the water was lukewarm and it just made me more sleepy..."

"...The showers are out of service right now."

This was only a temporary base for the Federacy, so the facilities were relatively insufficient. Either way, she looked up at Shin, who was still half asleep, with a strained smile.

"Shin... Did you get lost?"

After all, this place wasn't anywhere between the showers and Shin's room. This comment made Shin look around with his eyes still half-closed.

"...Where is this?"

Figures.

"I'll take you back to your room, follow me."

And so Shin let her pull him by the hand like a child (apparently he wasn't thinking at all, given that he was nodding off as they walked), and when they got to his room, Lena put him to bed. And though there was no need to do so, Lena got carried away by this moment of responsibility, and tucked him in.

"I'll come wake you up when it's time for dinner… Good night."

So she said, and made to leave…but in her elation she failed to consider the showers were broken that day and only produced tepid water, which meant Shin was cold after taking a shower. And when people are cold and tired on top of it, they instinctively seek warmth—and are thus naturally likely not to let go of any source of warmth right in front of them.

And so, her arm was grabbed, and before she knew it she was pulled down onto the bed.

"Huh?"

Shin hugged Lena—who was stunned in amazement—and fell asleep.

"Huuuuuuuh?!"

Hearing her story to the end, Annette narrowed her eyes at Lena like a disgruntled cat.

"So, he basically used you as a hot-water bottle… How are you getting out of this one?"

"I-it's the showers' fault for breaking down and not doing their role properly. I have to punish the showers first…!"

"…You're really panicked, aren't you? Forget that, figure out how to get out of here first."

"I mean, yes, but if I move, I might wake him up…"

She couldn't see Shin since he was hugging her and had his head down, but she could hear him breathing serenely. He finally got some deep sleep in, so it felt wrong to free herself and stir him awake.

"Uh-huh… Yes, and you're sure that's your only reason? You don't feel like it'd be a waste to leave, do you?"

"W-well…"

Frederica walked in wordlessly and roughly threw a blanket over them before spreading it out. This made Shin's grasp on Lena slacken—probably because he got warmer—freeing her.

"Th-thank you… Phew…" Lena sank to the floor, her cheeks red.

The two girls looked down on him and sighed. Thankfully, as Frederica casually confirmed the following day, Shin didn't remember any of this.

A Shadow Cast Over the Cup

The full moon cast its light brightly over the ruins. Faint red petals of countless cherry blossoms basked in its glow. This area was one of the Republic's eastern front's first defensive ward's first defensive unit, Spearhead's, sectors. These ruins were a main street covered in rubble. The cherry blossom trees planted on each side of the road were in full bloom, and the Republic's wide streets were covered by this canopy of pink.

Looking up more closely, flower petals fell from their branches and fluttered down from the trees, dancing in the blue moonlight. There was no wind, and it was a silent spring night, with all the wildlife fast asleep. This made the clouds of pale-pink flowers creeping through the silent, moonlit dark look like some kind of vile monster.

A monster that snatches away the hearts of men for all eternity.

Sitting at the back of his Juggernaut—which took him here and climbed atop an appropriately elevated pile of rubble—Shin looked up, taking in the silence and serenity of the place. Doing a flower viewing and looking up at these hidden cherry blossoms was Kaie's idea. Admiring the flowers and sipping on liquor—it was an Orienta tradition from her ancestral homeland. A spring tradition of her people, who celebrated the turning of the seasons.

Having been born and raised in the Republic, Kaie didn't know much more about the tradition, but she somehow managed to find some appropriate Orienta cups, to keep up the atmosphere. Since Shin was used to drinking out of metal cups, the strange, flat cups she brought felt superlight in his hand. They were carved out of wood and had a special coating applied to them. This black coating, called lacquer, had a distinctive sheen that drew the eye, and the shadow of the flowers hung over the clear liquor in the cup.

He took a sip. The alcohol burned in his throat, and the mellow flavor filled his mouth. It felt like recently he was learning to appreciate the sweetness of grains. After emptying his glass, Matthew breathed out and spoke. He had the thick blond hair of a L'asile and the bluish-purple eyes of an Iola. He had a tall, tempered physique reminiscent of a snow leopard.

"Good."

Even Shin—who, taciturn as he was, thought Matthew was a man of too few words—smiled at the Spearhead squadron's gunner's concise impression.

"Looking for it was worth it, then."

"I've never tasted anything like it before, but I think it's good."

"It makes me feel kinda flighty," Mina said as she held the small cup with both hands.

She laughed, her hazel braids swaying. Despite her petite, young appearance, she served as a vanguard.

"...Are you bad with booze? Don't drink too much, then," Kujo said with a sarcastic smile as he downed his own cup.

Kujo was the gentle giant sort of person with a large build, and would scribble a countdown to the end of his service—the end of their lives—on the blackboard in the hangar. Unlike Mina, his younger sister figure, he was good with alcohol.

"Miiiight be too late for that. You're kinda spinning, Kujo..."

"Gimme a break..."

"Ehee-hee."

"Well, you're probably better than them, they're already pretty far gone," Kaie said with a strained smile, gesturing with her eyes past the boulevard of cherry blossom trees.

Running around and dancing a weird dance in a clearly intoxicated manner were Daiya, Haruto, Kino, and Touma. Their other squad members, both boys and girls, were mingling with each other and having fun. As Chise tried to avoid attention, Kuroto pulled him by the hand, forcing him to join in on the dance. Everyone let out a slightly louder "Whoa!"

They were clearly cutting loose, as the saying goes, but even Kaie, who came up with this idea so her tense squad mates could get a chance to relax a little, was getting mixed feelings about this.

"Flower watching is supposed to be about appreciating the flowers, not a chance to get drunk and slack off… Besides, didn't they get drunk a little too fast? I get that they're not used to drinking… Or, well, that it's their first time drinking at all, but still."

Since they were branded as livestock and had to eat tasteless, dry, synthesized rations, the Eighty-Six weren't delivered any kind of luxuries.

"Well, if they're having fun, just let them."

"Earlier you said you don't care, Shin. I've been meaning to tell you this, but people can tell when you're not being honest."

She frowned her lips, a shade of pink just slightly thicker from the petals above them, but then smiled wryly.

"But it really is fun. Everyone gathering like this, having fun, fooling around. We've been fighting for years, but times like these…"

In between skirmishes, in small moments of reprieve. Small exchanges about nothing in particular, trivial little everyday events. They could still enjoy the time they spent with their friends.

Kujo exclaimed, with a face that was slightly flushed, "You bet! After all, the moment you stop laughing is when you lose!"

"Right!" Mina, who'd been frolicking with his large frame, cheerfully raised her hands up to the sky. She looked thoroughly drunk. Past her, Shin could see Matthew crack an uncharacteristic smile. Daiya and Haruto stopped their silly dance and approached.

"Oh, what's up? Did you call for us?"

Their cheeks were slightly red. Their voices were slightly relaxed. They had smiles plastered on their faces and wobbled on their feet a bit. They were clearly drunk off their first experience with alcohol. Kaie, who was seated and situated lower, looked up at them and frowned.

"We were just talking about how loud you were."

"Oh, come on." Daiya waved a hand dismissively. "Things like this just get you pumped up, you know? Festivals and stuff!"

"If anything, I gotta ask why you and Shin are sitting here all serious like. Come on, have some fuuun and stuff! Yaaay!"

But after saying this in a jovial manner, Haruto then said with oddly sober eyes, "Ah, actually, no. I take that back, sorry. Shin and Matthew, don't party like that. Even if you want to, don't. It'll be like, hell freezing over, some herald of the end times."

""Yay,"" Shin and Matthew said in unison, their voices blank of emotion.

"Yeah, thanks. Now stop," Haruto cut into their words.

Kujo cracked up laughing. Mina started cackling, too, but it was hard to tell if she actually listened to them or not. Daiya then crossed his arms and looked up diagonally.

"But really, I wish there was something else that would get everyone excited, you know? Like a snowball fight...or like, a cherry blossom fight, or something? Or maybe a treasure hunt under the cherry blossom trees!"

"Nah, just enjoy the cherry blossoms," Kujo said.

"Oh, come on. I mean, they're pretty, but it doesn't have that *whoa, this is fun* factor."

"Meow."

"...Right, I forgot about the cat," Matthew muttered.

Haruto pouted, displeased to have had his comment ignored.

"Well, they say there are corpses under cherry blossom trees," Shin said with a grin. "Not exactly a buried treasure."

"For real?!"

Daiya and Haruto looked strangely excited by that comment.

"That's it! Let's look for that!"

"Kino, Kinoooo. Didja bring some shovels? Enough for all of us!"

"Why would I bring a shovel? Are you stupid?"

"We gotta find shovels! Then we can race to see who digs one up first!"

"Hey, Daiya, hold up! No head starts!"

With that said, Daiya and Haruto, with Kino tagging along, raced off outside the cherry blossom boulevard.

Seeing them off, Kaie dropped her shoulders. "Those guys…"

"Ah!" Mina suddenly got to her feet. "Did you see that, Kujo?! A shooting star!"

"No, you probably imagined it, Mina… Ah, hold on, don't run off after it! What are you, a kid?!"

As Mina took off, chasing the shooting star, Kujo got to his feet to go after her. He raised his hand apologetically at Kaie and Shin and followed Mina, who was hopping away like a little rabbit. Matthew got to his feet, too, a faint smile on his lips.

"I'll go help him."

Saying this, he followed those two with quick steps. Their uniformed figures vanished one by one into the dark of night under the cherry blossom trees.

"…"

Chise, dizzy from being played around, walked past the trees with wobbly steps, too. Kuroto followed in a bit of a hurry. They both turned around, waved at Kaie and Shin for a second, and disappeared between the tall, black trees. Everyone went there, alone or in pairs, one after another. Under the cherry blossoms with their cups in hand, the Spearhead squadron members got to their feet, laughed, and walked off. The shrill voices of the girls as they chased the fluttering flowers disappeared beyond the trees with a wave of their hands. Two child soldiers walked away, seeing the flowers off with an imitated salute.

One by one. One after another, into the night, into the unknowable, into the dark. Just like how their time will eventually come to an end.

Before long, the laughter echoing through the flower-lit darkness died down, giving way to silence. Kaie, the last one left beside him, sipped on the sake in her cup elegantly.

"…It's good. I'm surprised you actually found rice sake from the Orient. Did you go looking for it?"

"Yeah. I thought we may as well go with that."

Kaie decided to use these cherry blossoms they found deep in the battlefield as a place to make some final memories, so Shin decided to find some of this alcohol, to let her taste the flavor of the homeland she never knew, where her ancestors came from.

Even if, to the very end, she never would have experienced it.

"Thank you. It's a bit of a shame… I can't say it brings back memories."

The Eighty-Six were born in the Republic and raised on the battlefield. They knew nothing but the battlefield and, without ever knowing anything else, they all passed on.

Holding the empty cup before her chest like a tribute, Kaie smiled.

"…In the country where my ancestors were born, you can't drink alcohol until your twenty-first birthday. So drinking this today is kind of cheating."

Shin chuckled. That was something Kaie would say, serious girl that she was.

"You're already older than that."

"You think…? Maybe. I was eighteen two years ago, but I don't remember what my birthday is anymore."

After being cast out into the Eighty-Sixth Sector, into the harsh, difficult conditions of the internment camp and the battlefield, one's ability to keep track of the date became hazy. The families that would celebrate their birthdays were gone before they knew it, and so the Eighty-Six rarely remembered their own birthdays.

This was true of Shin, at least, and Kaie was likely the same. They'd forgotten the date of their births by the time—if not long before—the faces of their parents and siblings and the visage of their homeland became distant memories.

However—

"—April 7th."

Kaie's eyes widened with disbelief at Shin's words. Looking straight at her, Shin continued sincerely.

"After the Republic fell, the Processors' personnel files were discovered in the army headquarters. There was mine, Raiden's, the whole squad's."

They should have been disposed of after their deaths, since the

Eighty-Six were not afforded graves or any way of leaving their names in the world, and yet a record of their existence remained.

"Using that, we could find out the names of our families and where we used to live, at least in wide terms. And that includes our dates of birth. As for the houses, looking at them now, they just look like unfamiliar houses at this point."

Now that the Federacy Army retook Liberté et Égalité's first ward, Shin did go to see his old home once.

"...Is that why you came here today? Now, in April, in the season of the cherry blossoms?"

"That's part of it. But..."

He wanted to celebrate it. That they were born into this world, grew older and matured, surviving until their last moment. That they truly existed. On Kaie's birthday, which was closest to when their unit was formed, with everyone. That was part of it, too.

But more than anything...

"I still remember you. I won't forget. I felt like I had to tell you this, one more time."

He promised to remember the comrades who fought with him and died before he did, to take them to their final destination. That was his duty as their reaper.

He needed to tell them that he hadn't discarded that duty yet. That he hadn't forgotten them. Since the Eighty-Six were afforded no grave markers, his comrades from the Spearhead squadron were slumbering even now, here in the first defensive ward's battlefield that, in a way, served as their graveyard.

And now, he set foot here again, alive.

"Right..." Kaie cast down her eyes and smiled faintly. "You were... Right, you were born in May. You're almost my age, even though you were younger than me two years ago."

"Yeah."

"That's a bit frustrating. But..."

Kaie smiled at him in that moment—brightly, from the bottom of her heart.

* * *

"I really am glad you guys managed to survive."

Those words were spoken not just with Kaie's voice. It was hers, and Daiya's and Haruto's and Kino's and Kujo's and Matthew's and Mina's—the voice of all of them who died before him.

"Yeah."

The wind gusted. Cherry blossoms had a very brief lifespan. It was this fragility, this transience reflected in their color, that stood for how they bloomed all at once and fell together.

They left their branches and scattered to the ground, without regrets or reluctance.

This was why they were loathed as ominous flowers by soldiers and warriors who swore to return from battle. And why they were loved as flowers of nobility and courage by soldiers who set out into the field of battle, knowing they would never return.

The flowers scattered, countless petals at the height of their bloom blown in the wind. Light as feathers, they rode the nighttime wind, frolicking in the air and dyeing it in their color without touching down on the soil.

This was called a cherry blossom blizzard.

Petals blew into the air, enough of them to dye everything over, riding the wind in a swirl as they covered the main street in their faint pink color. The curtain of these colors covered all, over the bottomless darkness Kaie and his comrades all vanished into—

"Captain Nouzen?"

That voice he'd gotten used to hearing over the last month, along with the pure fragrance of violets. Turning around, he saw Lena standing under the shower of cherry blossoms clad in her blue Republic uniform, her silver Celena hair the same color as her eyes.

Looking ahead again, there was no one standing under the blooming cherry blossom trees. Sitting atop the rubble they had used as a makeshift table, opposite Shin, was a single untouched cup full of sake. The ones who were to pick up and drink that cup were there no longer. They'd been gone for two years now.

Lena walked across the cracked pavement, the heels of her pumps clicking loudly with each step. The elegant, superior fragrance of her perfume ill-fitted these ruins that stood abandoned for eleven years.

They were currently deployed to the old Republic territory—she as tactical commander and he as the armored unit's total operations commander for the Eighty-Sixth Strike Package. They were currently stationed at a provisional base near the front lines, not far from the first defensive ward where Shin once served as captain of the Spearhead squadron.

He knew this was a violation of regulations, but he slipped away to the battlefield all alone under cover of night.

"I was surprised when you disappeared from the base's barracks all of a sudden…even if I knew you'd be able to tell there's no Legion here."

"Sorry. I was going to head back, so I figured I wouldn't have to tell you."

Saying this, Shin got to his feet, placing the empty cup in his hands in front of the untouched one.

"I'm surprised you found me here, though. I thought you didn't know about this place, Colonel."

She never came here, of course, nor did he ever tell her about it or even Resonate with her through the Para-RAID here.

"Your unit's mechanic, Sergeant Guren, told me your Juggernaut was missing. The sergeant didn't know where you went, so I asked First Lieutenant Shuga where you might be."

"…I'm pretty sure I asked them both to stay quiet about this."

He looked ahead, finding Raiden—who probably gave Lena a ride here on his unit—shrugging at him. Guren was one thing, but Raiden knew full well what Shin was doing here, so he expected him not to rat him out. The fact that he brought her over implied that Lena really pressured him with her questioning.

Ignorant of the two Processors's hair-raising glaring contest, Lena looked up to the starry sky covered in cherry blossoms. She let out a breath of amazement.

"...It's pretty."

"Yes... It was pretty last time, too. Two years ago, about this time of year."

As her argent eyes looked up at him, Shin didn't gaze back at them this time.

"We did a flower viewing here, all of us at the Spearhead squadron. Two years ago, right after we got assigned to the first ward."

Eighty-Sixers who outlived their usefulness were always stationed at a final disposal site to ensure they died in battle. At the end of their six months of service at that site, their death was assured.

"It was Kaie's idea, and it was all twenty-four of us. But back then..."

Looking at the faint-pink petals that seemed to shine in the dark, Shin narrowed his eyes. Most of the people who were here to watch these flowers back then are gone now, but the blooming cherry blossoms, the moon, and the dark of night hadn't changed.

"We had to drink water from these cups."

Most of the squadron didn't know that drinking water out of sake cups was a sign of farewell.

"I'm sorry... I interrupted you here, didn't I?"

"No, I'm mostly finished."

Visiting the graves of his comrades, who had no grave markers.

"Let's go back," Shin said.

Lena nodded, silently complying. She glanced at the two cups sitting on the rubble, but didn't say a word. Instead, she sniffed the air and looked at him pensively.

"...Something smells nice."

Shin raised his hand, showing off a ceramic bottle—meant for sake—that he had brought along with the cups.

"You want to try it? We can drink some when we get back to base. There isn't much left, though."

"This is...sake, yes?"

"Orienta sake, it's called. It's where Kaie came from."

"...I'm surprised you found something like this. The Federacy barely restored trade with other countries, right?"

Much like the Republic, the Federacy spent years with its territory closed off by the Legion armies, and only recently did it confirm the survival of some neighboring countries. Travel between the countries was limited to just a small trickle of people. The survival of the Far Eastern countries was yet to be confirmed, to speak nothing of any diplomatic relations with them.

There would be no reason, then, to expect goods from that country to find their way to the Federacy. This meant Shin must have gone around the department stores and antique shops in Sankt Jeder to find these things. Or, at worst, used something else as a substitute for the real thing.

"There's a winery in the south of the Federacy that makes these things on the side. There's no demand for them in the Federacy, so while they're rare, they're not sold for much, and the brewers mostly do it as a hobby."

The shop clerk had recalled that this set was collecting dust on one of the shelves and brought it over for Shin.

Lena cracked a sarcastic smile. "So this is why everyone was so loud in the dining hall when I left the base."

In terms of size, it followed Orienta traditions, making the sake bottle twice as large as the one used for Federacy wine and liquor. He only poured the amount of sake that would be necessary for this trip and shared the rest with his squad mates, who wasted no time in enjoying it.

Federacy military regulations did not forbid alcohol consumption so long as it was outside active duty hours, and since Shin's ability told him there were no Legion in the area, they could relax without a care in the world.

"Maybe I'll share in it, too, then... By the way," Lena said and then loudly cleared her throat.

She thrust a finger before Shin, who looked back at her in surprise and smiled impishly.

"You were driving under the influence, Captain Nouzen."

Shin couldn't help but let out a strained smile. "I didn't drink enough to get drunk. Plus, Aquilans are strong drinkers, from what I hear."

This was something Ernst—a Jet, meaning another sub-family of Aquila like Shin—told him. Since the Aquilans were a warrior class in ancient times, they had a resistance to all manner of drugs, including alcohol. And indeed, Shin—who had part Onyx blood—and Raiden—who was a pure-blooded Eisen—were unusually tolerant of alcohol.

Lena, however, stuck to her teasing attitude.

"Are you sure? Maybe I should ask Raiden to tow your unit away?"

"Never."

"Leave me out of this," Raiden grumbled behind them, only to be ignored by both.

Incidentally, in both the Republic and the Federacy, driving after drinking alcohol wasn't illegal so long as one wasn't inebriated enough to have their judgment impaired.

"Are you even allowed to drink at your age, Captain? I mean, legally speaking, in the Federacy."

"The legal drinking age is sixteen, I think, so it should be fine. I'm two years older than that."

"What's your birthday, by the way?"

"May...something, if I recall correctly."

He didn't care much for his date of birth, so he didn't remember it properly.

"Captain, why do you have to be so...?" Lena dropped her shoulders in exasperation and sighed. "Well, we'll be going back to the Federacy soon. Once we get back, look into it again. And report it to me."

"...I don't mind, but why?"

"Isn't it obvious?" Lena said and smiled like a blooming flower. "We'll all celebrate together... All right?"

HELP! (Shin's POV)

Aquilans were typically strong against the effects of alcohol. Shin was no exception, and hardly ever got drunk. Raiden, who was also Aquilan, was likewise a strong drinker. Anju and Theo had decent alcohol tolerance, albeit not on the same level as an Aquilan. Kurena was the weakest drinker, and even she could drink enough to remain sober during social occasions.

As such, Shin never knew that some people out there couldn't hold their liquor after just a glass or two.

And now, he was being scolded from point-blank range.

"Captain Nouzen! Are you listening to me?!"

He was not. Namely because he was in no position to be listening to anything.

As Lena looked down at him, standing much too close for comfort, Shin looked back at her. Her face was flushed with intoxication, which made him break into a cold sweat.

They were the same age, but given they were a boy and girl in their late teens, they had a 15 cm height difference. In a normal conversation, Lena would not be looking down at Shin.

Not in a *normal* conversation.

Because right now, they were in a shared bedroom for four in their stationed base, and Lena was pushing him down onto a bed. What's more, she was grabbing both of his wrists with her knees on both sides of his body, making it difficult to move. Raiden was peering into the room with an expression that was half shocked, half fed up.

"...What are you doing?"

"Help me."

"Thanks for the treat."

What?

"I mean, what's the problem? Have your treat."

"You know I can't do that."

What is he even on about?

"...Shin, I think you're blurting out what you're actually thinking right now. Are you really shaken up?" said Theo, who was also peering into Shin's room.

"You could tell something was wrong when he, of all people, asked for help," Raiden said, and sighed. "So, what got you in this fun position?"

"This isn't fun… Remember how I went to sit down with Kaie after dinner today? There was a little Orienta sake left after that…"

This camp they were stationed in for a few days was close to the Eighty-Sixth Sector's first ward. Shin went to the first ward's burial site where his comrades slumbered with Orienta sake in hand shortly before he found himself in this predicament.

The squadron's Processors had drunk most of the sake in the bottle, and Lena was interested in the rest. When they returned to base, their tipsy squad mates were partying, so Shin figured he'd have her try the sake somewhere more quiet, and took her to his room.

That was a fatal mistake.

Hearing his story, Raiden snorted tiredly.

"Just push her away, man."

"I'd do that if we weren't in this room, in this position, and this situation…!"

Even with all her body weight on him, Lena was light, while Shin had been raised on the battlefield. He could easily push her off. However, this was a frontline base. The rooms and beds were all the bare minimum in terms of function, meaning the place was extremely cramped.

Pushing Lena off would mean knocking her off the bed. If his hands were free, he could have grabbed her and moved her away, but both of his hands were sewn to the bed by Lena's lithe fingers. Trying to forcibly shake her off would knock Lena off balance. Her eyes were visibly unfocused and her small, silver head was already clearly spinning. Trying to move her too hard could get her injured, which meant Shin was effectively barred from moving.

"Ah… Well, uh, you know. They say not reaching for your meal when the woman sets it out for you is shameful."

"What part of this strikes you as a 'prepared meal' exactly?! No matter how you look at this, this is just an explosive situation!"

"I mean, you do realize that looking at the circumstances, you took her to your room, got her drunk, and forced yourself on her, right?"

"Forced myself…?!"

Ignoring Shin's shocked response, Raiden turned to Shiden, who was standing in the hall.

"Shiden, this is pretty funny, so give them thirty minutes and come pick up Lena then."

"...Fine, I guess... Can he last thirty minutes, though? In more ways than one."

"From the looks of it, I think Lena's the one who won't last thirty minutes, so I'm sure it'll be fine... Ah."

As they were talking, Lena exhausted all her strength and toppled over—with Shin naturally pinned under her.

"Wait...!" Shin let out a nondescript scream, but they ignored him, with Shiden mercilessly shutting the door.

But of course, Shiden did soon come to help him out of pity. And, fortunately enough, when Raiden checked on Lena the following day, he found she didn't remember anything.

May 19th (Shin's Birthday)

We'll all celebrate together—Lena certainly did say that. However...

"...It ended up landing on our next mission," Annette said, sipping on her mug of coffee substitute.

"Yes...," Lena said, sitting across from her and looking visibly dejected.

May 19th. Shin's Birthday. His forgotten date of birth was discovered in the records recovered from the Republic, and Lena was intent on celebrating it. But sitting now in the Rüstkammer base officers' club—mostly empty during daytime—Lena was sprawled against a single-seat sofa's armrest like a dainty white flower battered by the rain.

As she thought that she couldn't let her subordinates see her like this, Lena watched Annette pick up a biscuit. Both the hazelnuts and the precious rare cocoa used to make it were real products of the south, making it exceptionally tasty.

"You're deployed to the United Kingdom, right? And close to the front lines, at that."

They were informed the Strike Package would be deployed abroad for the entirety of May, including Shin's birthday, meaning celebration would be impossible.

"We are soldiers, after all... That's something we should be prepared for..."

"What you're saying doesn't match the expression on your face, Lena."

Lena was so sad that, if she was a kitten, her ears and tail would certainly be drooping.

"...And I mean, would you even have celebrated it even if we weren't deploying? You haven't spoken to Shin much recently."

"Well...," Lena muttered, becoming even more dispirited.

Annette heard the gist of Lena's conversation with Shin on their way back to base from the Republic. She also knew that, needless to say, things had been awkward between Lena and Shin ever since. So, while it was a bit forced, she did think the birthday was a good excuse to get them to talk again—Annette pondered it as she dipped a second biscuit into her coffee.

Another idea was to snap a photo of Lena's current dejected appearance and send it over to Shin. That would make for a nice present. She had been able to come to terms with her relationship with her old childhood friend to the degree that she was capable of pulling these kinds of pranks. She'd more or less come to accept the idea of Shin as a colleague and nothing more.

"But still, it's not just Shin; all of the Eighty-Six forgot their birthdays, so they've never celebrated them. And when their birth dates were discovered, nothing was ever really done with the information, right? I don't think they'll mind even if they don't get to celebrate."

The clerks in the Federacy were in a very foul mood when the tentative birth dates for the Eighty-Six's personnel files had to be updated and the Eighty-Six themselves never even came to check. They were planning to celebrate birthday parties for every single one of them (meaning it would be every single day of the year, since there were several thousand in the Strike Package).

Since a birthday party every day would be logistically impossible, Grethe set a system where, on the first of every month, they would celebrate birthdays for everyone born that month. This was exceptionally hard on Shin and Kurena, who had May birthdays.

"The fact they don't mind is what bothers me!" Lena leaned forward. "...It's exactly because they didn't have the time to care about it until now that I want them to feel like celebrating is natural... Or, well, that was my plan..."

Lena became dispirited again. Annette honestly thought she was being a drag at the moment, and so said, "Why not just get him a present for the time being?"

"Eh?"

"You bought him one before you got in that fight, right? You got presents for Shin, Second Lieutenant Kukumila, and for Second Lieutenant Rikka, too, even though his birthday was a month ago. You went to the next town over and spent the whole day looking for gifts."

Annette imagined that the bulk of that time was spent on one person in particular, but she wasn't expecting Lena to be fair in where she divided her attention.

"But, erm...the captain's busy getting ready for the expedition..."

Lena started fidgeting.

Feeling thoroughly fed up with her, Annette decided to play her hand. After all, if Lena wasn't going to give her a present, Annette couldn't give Shin the present she got him on the pretext that Lena bothered her about it.

"Fine, then since you're so gutless, your best friend forever has a brilliant idea for you... Wanna hear it?"

God, why am I such a nice friend?

"Captain Nouzen, I'm here to deliver something you dropped. Must be yours, as no one else here reads these complicated books."

"Hm? Oh, thanks."

The corporal in charge of lost articles, who didn't usually show up to make deliveries personally, suddenly thrust a hardcover book that was found lying abandoned in the break room, and left.

While Shin did read books, it was always just a distraction from the Legion's voices. He could only assume the cat had moved the book out of sight, or Frederica put it there as a prank.

"...Mm?"

However, Shin realized something was wrong and opened the book. It opened at a certain page. Stuck between the pages was not a piece of paper used as a bookmark, but a thin, long paper plate with meticulous fretwork—a metallic bookmark.

When he picked it up, an embossed card sandwiched under it fell out of the hardcover. It had the faint, familiar scent of violet. Written in heliotrope ink were letters in the elegant, cursive handwriting he'd gotten used to seeing over this last month—as well as two years ago.

Apparently, she had it made-to-order, and it had a pattern of a licorice flower with a Juggernaut standing beside it.

Let's celebrate next year... Happy birthday.

"...It's a bit early, Lena. It's still two weeks away."

He realized that she had to do this now, as they'd be on the battlefield in two weeks. With that thought in mind, Shin snapped the book shut. He could only hope that come July...they'd be back at their base and able to celebrate the birthday of a certain someone who just scampered off on the other end of the hallway, probably thinking she wasn't spotted.

May 6th (Kurena's Birthday)

"Kurena, it's a bit belated, but...happy birthday."

"Th-thanks."

Kurena excitedly accepted the small box Lena handed her. A birthday. She couldn't remember how many years it had been since she last celebrated her birthday. She'd…completely forgotten about it, honestly. No one had the time or need to celebrate birthdays in the Eighty-Sixth Sector.

"Can I open it?"

"Of course. I just hope you like it."

Opening the long, thin, velvet box, she found a gleaming gold pendant. It had a thin golden chain that matched Kurena's tan, sun-kissed skin, and was inlaid with a pretty orange stone.

Kurena had to hold back a gasp of amazement. A long time ago… she hardly remembered it now, but her mother and big sister, whom she adored and admired, wore accessories a lot like it. It twinkled in the light and looked mature and womanly.

"It's beautiful…" The words slipped from Kurena's lips.

Lena smiled in relief. "I'm glad you like it."

"Yeah, I…I like it. Ah, erm!" Kurena realized something and asked a question. Since she just got a present, it only made sense to repay the favor. "When's your birthday? And—wait."

Kurena herself didn't remember her own birthday, and with her parents and sister dead, there was no one left to remember it. So, of course, no one would know to celebrate it.

"How do you even know my birthday…?"

"Shin."

When she stopped Shin in the hall, he was carrying a thick book he'd lost a while ago and apparently lost interest in under his arm. It had a silver bookmark gleaming between its pages, one she didn't remember him having.

"Did something nice happen, Kurena?"

"Eh?"

"You just look happy… You're smiling."

Shin said this with a serene smile, which Kurena had never seen him with, either. She pondered over how he had started smiling more lately. Two years ago, back when they were in the Eighty-Sixth Sector and death was a forgone conclusion, he was much more strained when having to look at that fate in the eyes. Compared to that, he was more peaceful now.

"Yeah… Just a little something."

Maybe it was because she was a year younger, but Shin always seemed to treat her like a little sister. And while she was happy he saw her as a sister rather than just another member of the squadron, she didn't want to be seen as just that.

She had no intention of voicing her dissatisfaction, but a part of her lamented the fact that their age gap was just one more thing that kept them apart. She desperately wanted to reach his level. She wanted him to acknowledge her as an equal.

However, Kurena's birthday was May 6th, while Shin's was May 19th. Kurena had just turned seventeen a few days ago. And, while Shin was a year older than her and set to turn eighteen this year, it was still a few days before the nineteenth, meaning he was still seventeen years old.

For just some ten odd days, they were the same age. Being the same as him, even if only for a short while, made Kurena happy. It gave her the feeling that, for just a little bit, she could stand in the same place as this person she could otherwise never catch up to.

Seeing Kurena look at him with an oddly forlorn smile of joy, Shin exclaimed like he just remembered something.

"Wasn't it your birthday? Oh… Sorry, it's past that already, right?"

"No, it's fine. I know you've been busy."

The Strike Package's first armored group, which Kurena was a part of, was to be deployed to their next battlefield, the United Kingdom of Roa Gracia, in two weeks. As the armored group's commander, Shin was incredibly busy with preparations.

"…Still." Shin frowned.

They'd forgotten their birthdays and thought they were inconsequential, but Shin still felt that if they knew their birthdays, they were worth celebrating. And so, Kurena said with a smile—giving him a helping hand, like an equal; like a spoiled little sister—

"If you feel that way, Shin, you should get me a cake in the dining hall. A chocolate cake."

"I don't mind, but…are you sure that's all you want?"

"You have to eat a slice, too."

"Erm…"

She spoke her whim knowing he was bad with sweets, and indeed, Shin looked put on the spot. Kurena looked up at him with a giggle.

86

[EIGHTY-
SIX]

THE UNITED KINGDOM OF ROA GRACIA ARC

They spent their adolescence there, on the battlefield.

EIGHTY-SIX

Life, land, and legacy. All reduced to a number.

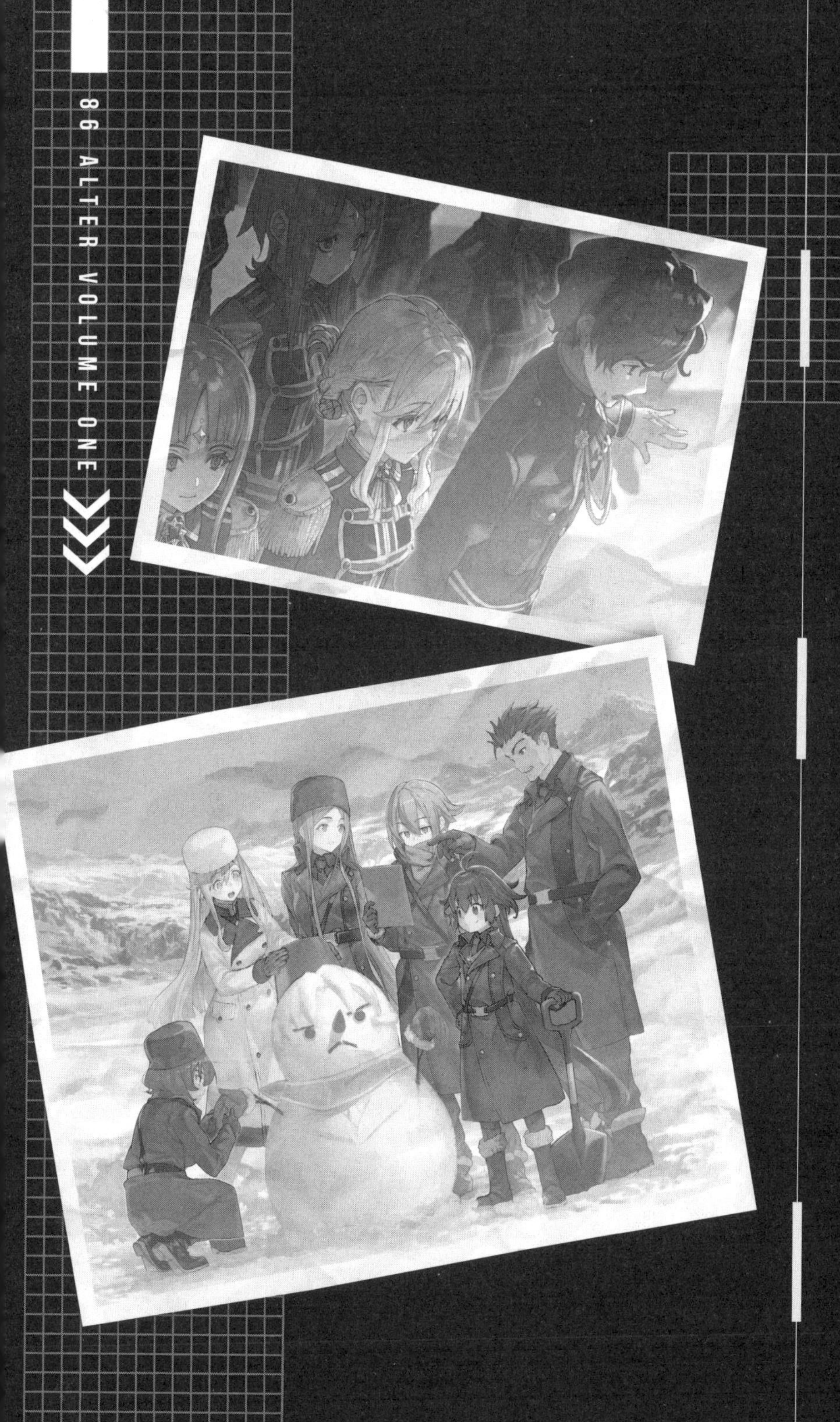
86 ALTER VOLUME ONE

86

[EIGHTY-SIX]

THE UNITED KINGDOM OF ROA GRACIA ARC

Chess

Since the Revich Citadel Base was underground...or rather, built into the rock, the limited space there was mostly taken up by Feldreß and their exchange parts, with the personnel being forced into what little space was left. People were only given the bare minimum space needed to live.

That was why several dining halls in the base were also used as lounges during free time. The third dining hall was the one the Strike Package's Processors and maintenance crew gathered in. They reached a tacit understanding with the United Kingdom soldiers about which army occupied which spot, though apparently the United Kingdom soldiers still walked in every now and then with sweets or alcohol in hand.

When Lena entered the dining hall, she found Shin in one corner of the room—seated across from Vika, for some reason, with a chessboard between them.

The usual group—Raiden, Theo, Kurena, Anju, and Frederica—were all seated on chairs around them, along with Dustin, Marcel, Shiden, and Rito, all of them watching over this battle taking place over the chessboard.

Lena stood on tiptoe, peered at the board, and then frowned. Atop the old wooden checkered battlefield, the white pieces were at such an overwhelming disadvantage that Lena had to wonder how the game state ever got to this point. Lena couldn't help but comment on it—this looked thoroughly unfair.

"Vika, erm, can't you take it easy on him?"

"What are you saying, Queen?" Vika asked, still glaring at the chessboard.

"Lena, I'm not sure how, but my side is winning," Shin said, his eyes fixed dubiously on the board, too.

Lena examined the board again in disbelief.

Oh.

Indeed, looking at the board again, based on the pieces' positions, the white pieces were Vika's and the black pieces were Shin's. In other words, Vika was the one being thoroughly beaten. It wasn't like commanders were necessarily good at chess or active combatants were necessarily bad at it, but Vika was royalty. Chess was surely one of his pastimes. Since Shin grew up on the battlefield, he surely had less time and freedom to polish his skills.

"Shin, are you good at chess...?"

"I know how the pieces move and some opening tactics, but that's about it. I only played it every now and then in the Eighty-Sixth Sector to kill time."

So, apparently, he wasn't a particularly strong player.

"I don't know any opening moves. I do know how to move the pieces, though."

"...Believe it or not, the prince played himself into a Fool's Mate on his first round," Raiden mumbled to her.

A Fool's Mate meant getting a checkmate in two turns by a player opening a path to their king for their opponent's queen. Lena had never seen a person actually fall for that.

"Why are you so weak at chess...?"

"Because I don't care for it, of course. The idea of it being the pastime of royalty is absurd."

"Then why are you playing it now...?"

"When I came over here to look, Nouzen and Shuga were playing...," Vika said with disinterest as he pondered his next move. "It looked fun, so I figured I'd try."

"..."

The way his face looked when he said that reminded Lena of a child; a small child asking to join in with a group of unfamiliar children playing around. Kurena cocked her head, apparently having the same association in her mind.

"Your Highness, why don't you try snakes and ladders next time? You play with a bigger group, though."

"I don't know the rules for it, but if you don't mind."

"Oh, don't worry about the rules. It's more luck than anything."

"I, erm, doubt you'll do as badly as you do in chess. And it's not like Shin's strong at it, either."

"There are too many of us, though... Do we take turns?"

"Oh, you can count me out, then. I'll play something else. What games have we got?"

"I've got one where you pile up wooden sticks and need to pull them out one by one. Does that sound good?"

"...By the way, Vika. If you do that, you're going to get checkmated next move."

"What...?!" Vika leaned in to look at the board.

Everyone laughed cheerfully, like a group of children who didn't care if they knew this new kid or not.

Lena chuckled and said, "Me too. Let me play along."

A Little Longer, Just like This

Soon after retaking the Revich Citadel Base, the snowy fields surrounding it were as shadowed by snow clouds as ever, making it extremely cold. Lena only had her uniform blouse on with a Federacy coat along with her bare feet stuffed into her pumps. This offered her basically no protection from the cold.

A soft sneeze disturbed the silence of the snow for a moment, snapping Lena and Shin, to whom she was clinging, out of their thoughts.

"I-I'm sorry."

"No need to apologize...and really, if you're cold, you should head back."

"Yes... Whoa?!"

Lena, her face flushed, let go of him and made to turn away when her legs sunk into the snow, making her topple over. Shin hurriedly caught her arm and kept her from falling at the last second. Lena clung to him again out of reflex, too, leaving them in an odd posture that was just barely balanced.

Holding that position, Shin asked, "You didn't twist your ankle, did you?"

"I'm fine... Erm, I can't stand on my own, so... Whoaaa?!"

Not at all fine, Lena nearly fell over again, and Shin supported her once more. Her pumps were completely unfit for walking through snow, and the cold made her numb and her motions slow. The pressure of the siege piled on top of all that and, with the fighting over, all the tension left her body. Her knees were giving way, and she was by no means capable of walking now.

Seeing this, Shin seemed to make up his mind.

"...Lena, I'll hear your complaints later."

"What... Hiyaaaaa?!"

Lena let out a screech as Shin scooped her up into his arms. He held her up by her back and the back of her knees, with the coat wrapped around her—a bridal carry, as it's called. He then walked off in quick steps. He had the fast steps of an active combatant, quite different from Lena's.

"If you're feeling unsteady, feel free to hold on to me."

"Shin, erm!"

"I said you can complain later... If you keep talking, you might bite your tongue."

"..."

It seemed walking soundlessly through the snow while carrying someone was difficult even for Shin. She could hear the unfamiliar sound of his footsteps crunching through the snow. His physique was quite unlike Lena's feminine one, his skeleton and muscles much more solid, and she could faintly hear the thumping of his heart through his thick armored flight suit.

The fact that it felt serene struck her as a bit unfair. After all, her heart was racing, and Shin could surely feel it.

"...Erm, am I heavy?"

"Not really. Well, I guess you're heavier than a cat."

Yes, that much she could imagine, but still. His bloodred eyes didn't look at Lena's sulking expression...but Lena was unaware that he couldn't bring himself to look her in the face in this situation.

She looked away, hoping he wouldn't see how red her face was. Her argent eyes spotted Fido, who apparently came to check on them, in the distance. Some part of her did think that it would be better if it waited a bit further away.

Your Presence (Shin's POV)

Even after retaking the base, as the commander of the Strike Package's armored unit, Shin had several tasks to attend to. He needed to contact the diversion unit and touch base with them, eliminate any remaining hostiles within the base, receive reports and report to his superiors.

Once everything settled down and he returned to his room to change, he was already quite exhausted. The base was built into thick rock, meant to contain the heat rising from the earth, and it made the room so warm it was hard to believe it was snowing outside.

And perhaps because of this warmth, fatigue washed over him like a wave, making him a bit dizzy. There were no Legion in the area—not a single one that could pose a threat or open combat. For the first time in a while, he was able to confirm this because he couldn't hear the wailing of the Sirin, either, which were indistinguishable from the Legion.

"..."

He took off his armored flight suit—which felt heavier than usual today, in this moment—and put on the steel gray Federacy uniform, which Frederica had apparently brought to his room, judging by how it was folded in her distinctive way.

Moving about in the room made the air shift a little, and suddenly the stench of blood and decay reached his nostrils.

This was the scent of the dead troops that remained within the fortress during the siege, as well as the scent of the casualties from the attacking side. The diversion unit would return soon, and the stench of their dead would join the mix. The base's ventilation system was still being restored and was working at minimal capacity, so the stench would hang over the place for a while.

Not that it bothered Shin that much. His nose was used to this smell by now, and hardly even noticed it anymore. He was used to the stench of clotting blood and decaying human corpses, even the smell of freshly spilled blood and viscera, which wasn't hanging in the air right now.

He put on the dark undershirt of his uniform. He couldn't be bothered to tie the necktie, so he just buttoned the uniform up to his collar and took the necktie out of the jacket. Looking at it in the faint darkness, the Federacy military's red necktie looked like the blackish crimson of old blood.

He rarely undid his tie or opened his collar, not out of any obligation to military regulations, simply intending to keep his scar out of sight, but he honestly didn't like keeping either on. He shouldn't have felt this way, but every now and then, it made him feel suffocated again.

And when that happened, it reminded him of his brother's grip on his throat—the same grip that left this scar on him.

Shaking his head, he put on his jacket and made to do up its buttons, which were higher up than on a normal suit. But then a delicate floral fragrance blew away the stench of stagnant death hanging in the air.

The scent of spring flowers—particularly early spring, shortly after the passing of winter. It wasn't a natural floral scent, but one carefully mixed with multiple fragrances for the purpose of drawing attention; a cool, refreshing, sweet perfume.

Shin's eyes widened in surprise. It had to have been his uniform—it had the Strike Package's armband and the armored division's eight-legged horse badge, and his was the only one with the captain's rank insignia. And yet—

As the word slipped from his lips and his bloodred eyes blinked in surprise, he didn't notice how all the tension and aggression drained from his body, like he'd been pacified by a spell.

"...Why?"

Why did it smell of Lena's violet perfume...?

Your Presence (Lena's POV)

Even after retaking the base, as the tactical commander of the Strike Package, Lena had several tasks to attend to. Once those had all settled down somewhat, Lena sank into her chair in the commander room, where only Vika, Frederica, and Marcel remained. She was tired. Understandably so, given the battle that just took place. But then she realized something and got up.

"Oh, the uniform...!"

While using the Cicada, she had borrowed someone's jacket. It was a male's blazer in the Federacy military's steel gray color. With the fighting over, she had to return it to its owner.

"Hmm?" Frederica eyed her dubiously. "You wish to return it already?"

Saying this, Frederica's pale fingers pointed ahead. Lena looked in that direction, at the door to the command room, where Shin was, having changed out of his armored light suit into his service dress.

...Eh?

Lena's thoughts froze up as Vika casually moved from his spot, standing in a way that hid Lena from sight if one were to look through the entrance to the room. Since he, too, had a habit of muffling his footsteps, he did so quietly.

A *male's* blazer in the Federacy military's metal black color.

One that's too big for Lena, but not *too* big, the kind to fit a slightly tall and slender boy. And for some reason, having it only made her feel safe and reassured.

And that was because…

It was Shin's…?

"Ah—"

Realizing the situation, Marcel promptly hit the closing switch to the commander room's door.

"Nooooo!"

The door closed rapidly, almost like it was protesting the notion that a heavy blast door couldn't possibly close that fast. As soon as it shut, Lena's scream shook the command room.

As the Bloodstained Queen went very red in the face, Frederica smirked at her.

"Only now do you realize, imbecile?"

"Y-you tricked me, Frederica?!"

"Do not sully my good name, I did no such thing. I merely showed you some consideration given that the Serpent of Shackles decided to bully you."

"C-consideration…?"

"Or was I wrong? It seems to me that you took quite a liking to Shinei's uniform."

"D-don't say it! Nooo!"

Vika looked torn between shock and pity.

"To begin with, didn't you see the rank and branch insignia on it? How didn't you notice?"

It had the armored division's symbol of the eight-legged horse and a captain's rank insignia—a combination of symbols that only matched Shin out of everyone in the Strike Package.

"Wait… Does that mean all of you knew?!"

Vika nodded with indifference while Marcel averted his gaze uncomfortably.

"Yes, erm, I think…all of the communications personnel noticed."

"…?!"

Lena couldn't even find the strength to squeal anymore. She was so embarrassed she almost swooned right then and there.

"Frederica...!" Lena turned, her eyes full of tears, to look at the girl who looked back at her with an evil smirk. Surely she was allowed this bit of payback, right?

"I wish I could take a photograph of that expression and show it off to Shinei."

With Coffee and Tea

"That concludes my report, Colonel Milizé."

"Thank you, Captain Nouzen... Really."

Seated at a used desk in the room that served as her temporary office after retaking the fortress, Lena smiled tiredly at Shin. It was late at night, and past lights-out, but sadly, Shin, as commander of the Strike Package's armored unit and Lena, as its tactical commander, had plenty of work to do. Between all the reports and message exchanges, the two had little to no time to chat.

Lena got to her feet and stretched. She then poured something from a nearby pot into a paper cup and handed it to Shin.

"If you'd like...? You look a bit on edge."

"Yes..." Shin accepted the cup with a sigh. He was aware of how tense he was, but apparently it was so evident even Lena saw it. "Sorry."

"It's fine. It makes sense you'd be tired after such a hard battle. It's not your fault."

The paper cup she gave him was full of clear, reddish synthesized tea. It had a fragrance that faintly reminded Shin of medicine. This was the kind of instant tea provided in the Federacy military's combat rations.

Looking at it, Shin smiled. "I see you do know how to pour tea."

"Well, excuse you!" Lena frowned grumpily. "I can at least do that. And..."

But as she spoke, she seemed to realize something and her voice tapered off.

"I, erm, got the hot water in the kitchen. They boiled it for me."

She looked away from Shin, sulking. He chuckled, not realizing that this was the first natural smile he'd cracked since the siege battle ended. Seeing this, Lena smiled in relief. After waiting for the tea to cool to a drinkable temperature, Shin tasted it.

"How is it?" She asked curiously.

"...It's sweet. Very."

It was a bit much for Shin, who wasn't good with sweets. He even winced a little, which made Lena giggle. She sipped her cup, too, with the gesture of a bird drinking water.

"It really is sweet."

Since the United Kingdom's northern battlefield was intensely cold, its combat rations were designed to provide high caloric value. This extremely sweet tea was part of that.

"Apparently they mix jam into tea, here in the United Kingdom."

"I heard as much from the maintenance crew before the battle. They did say they don't do it in the center of the United Kingdom, but they use fruit, flowers, and boiled sugar for tea crackers."

"Is that right...? That's a shame."

She looked at the red liquid's surface with regretful eyes. Shin couldn't imagine trying to further sweeten this already oversweet tea. Frederica was one to put a lot of sugar in her tea, too, so he had to wonder if girls had different sweetness receptors.

"Which do you prefer, Shin? Coffee or tea?"

Shin cocked his head pensively. It wasn't exactly a preference per se, but...

"I'm more used to coffee. Well, it's coffee substitute either way, just like this tea."

Unlike tea substitute, which was produced synthetically in production plants, coffee in the Eighty-Sixth Sector had dandelions and chicory as a readily available substitute. This was perhaps the sole reason the Eighty-Six, Shin included, had a preference for coffee.

"Really... I guess I'm just used to the taste of tea substitute by now."

Lena smiled faintly. She, too, was around seven years old when the

Legion war broke out. At the time, she didn't like the bitterness of coffee or the astringent flavor of tea, and Shin didn't remember what he liked back then.

"...Someday, let's have real tea and coffee. And then...I'll ask you which you prefer again," Lena said with a smile, wrapping her hands around the paper cup and gazing into the red fluid with eyes that seemed to gaze into the distance. To pray.

"Because then, I'll be able to make you both."

Once, We Gazed Upon the Aurora Together

Having left the Revich base and returned to the royal castle, Vika was scheduled to go back to the front lines the following day. Since he'd spent most of the last seven years engaged with the Legion war, however, Vika felt no particular emotion at making these preparations to leave.

His room, while fancy, was empty and had little in the way of personal articles, and so he left it behind and opened the large window out to the terrace and its nighttime view.

Since the temperature didn't rise at night, the silver Eintagsfliege clouds were gone. Only at this time of day was the night sky visible—the hems of the night queen's dress, made of the fur of silver foxes and inlayed with specks of snow.

With the temperature so low, they won't be visible this time of year, will they? thought Vika. The freezing climate wouldn't allow for view of the early summer constellations

Lerchenlied.

No matter what silly argument they had or how offended she got, whenever he found it and told her about it, she would stop crying and lose track of time as she gazed at it. She was that kind of girl.

The girl named after the bird that heralds the coming of spring was one who loved winter, who loved the soul-freezing winters of the United Kingdom. A girl who loved this world so much...she even found something to love in this harsh season...

Who saw things differently even when she stood in the same places he did.

Would the time have come, had she still been alive, when she realized this and despaired over it? He would never know the answer to that question now.

Hearing someone step on the thin layer of snow, Vika moved his eyes to look. Standing modestly in the garden beneath him, in the shadows cast by the starlight, was a Emerōd woman in her forties. She was dressed in the uniform of the castle's servants. Her face was familiar. He didn't remember all too clearly, but he knew her for as long as he could remember.

"Martina."

This woman was once his wetnurse. Lerche's—Lerchenlied's mother.

"Prince Viktor. May the snow goddess bless you on the expedition you embark on tomorrow."

Having been thoroughly disciplined as a servant in the castle, Martina bowed like a doll, from the angle of her body down to the timing of it all. Vika shrugged.

"Yes, well. Next time, I'll try to at least not suffer a shameful loss and have to run with my tail between my legs."

"No, not at all… Please, return to us safely next time, as well. That is all that matters to me."

This time she went against castle etiquette, bowing so deeply it nearly looked like she was about to hit her head against the ground. Her voice was choked with tears.

It was the voice of his surrogate mother, the woman who was always there to greet him when he returned from the battlefield. She was like this when her daughter still lived…and when her daughter died, too.

"Your Highness, is she… Is Lerchenlied still of help to you?"

"…Yes."

He couldn't bring himself to tell her that her service this time was so loyal she sacrificed everything below the neck for him—*a second time*—in this battle.

Martina was a court lady who was close to his mother, Queen Mariana. When Queen Mariana died, leaving Vika behind, Martina was holding Lerche—then a newborn infant—in her arms. For that reason alone, this woman and her daughter's entire lives were bought off. In the end, her one daughter ended up being remade into a moving corpse fashioned in her image.

In Vika's eyes, Martina had every right to resent him, but in the seven years since Lerchenlied's passing, she had never shown so much as sign of spite toward him. Even though he took her daughter's remains with him into the battlefield again, right in front of her.

"Forgive me. I can't return your daughter just yet."

"No," Martina pursed her lips tightly and shook her head. "No. Children are always meant to eventually leave the nest, to take flight into worlds their parents can never know."

I am not wishing for her return, she said.

"She was simply quick to leave the nest, that is all. She left my arms to fly into yours, Your Highness. It is a pity, then...for had fate not been so cruel, she would have spent her entire life bestowed with that honor."

"..."

Vika was Amethysta royalty, while Lerche was... Martina's daughter, Lerchenlied, was an Emerōd commoner. She couldn't serve as his concubine, to say nothing of a lover.

House Idinarohk was the last remaining Amethysta bloodline that retained its Esper abilities, and it could not lose those abilities, no matter what. The purity of that bloodline couldn't be muddled by mixing with other colors for any reason—especially not for something as trivial as one prince's personal feelings.

"...Forgive me."

"There is nothing to apologize for, Your Highness. She would have wished for this... And so, all I can do is watch her go."

Watch her go, while praying that the small bird leaving her nest will find bliss in her journey.

THE REAPER'S OCCASIONAL ADOLESCENCE ARC

They spent their adolescence there, on the battlefield.

[EIGHTY-SIX]

Life, land, and legacy.
All reduced to a number.

86 ALTER VOLUME ONE

86

[EIGHTY-SIX]

THE REAPER'S OCCASIONAL ADOLESCENCE ARC

May 19th (Shin's Birthday) – Part 2

"…Mm."

Seeing the name and address on the parcel, Rei blinked. The Giadian Empire's capital of Sankt Jeder, and its sender…

"Marquis Nouzen… Grandfather."

Rei had never met him, since his parents had fled the Empire, but this was his paternal grandfather. Rei's father had sent letters periodically, but his grandfather never sent a reply, save for once. On Rei's birthday, he had sent him a picture book.

The fact that he sent his grandson a present was all well and good, but the contents of said picture book were quite eerie. As Rei frowned, his younger brother, who was hiding behind one of the house's pillars, peered at him and tottered over. He was interested in the package, but since the deliveryman was a stranger, he was a bit afraid of him.

"Grandfather?"

"Right, I guess you don't know him. That's Father's father… He, erm, lives in another country, so we can't see him."

Hearing this seemed to confuse Shin even further. He knew what grandpas were—his friend who would come over to play from the house next door, Rita, had silver hair, but grandpas were grown-ups with a different shade of silver in their hair and wrinkled skin.

Since the topic of grandparents never came up in their home, Shin thought that, just like "housekeepers" and "maids," this was something some households had and others didn't.

"I have a grandpa, too?"

"Yes, you do. Mother's father passed away already, but he was your grandpa, too… See?"

The parcel was addressed to Shin, so Rei assumed it was a birthday present. Honestly, he thought it would be best to give it to their father first, but Rei tore the package open and took out its contents.

As expected, it was a picture book. It was covered in black silk and a ribbon—which already made Rei think it was eerie—and had a headless skeletal knight on its cover.

I knew it would be this…, Rei thought with a frown.

It was the same picture book he had mailed to Rei some ten odd years ago. Reading it now, it was an interesting story, which seemed like a given, considering its protagonist was a headless skeleton knight. But when he was young, it looked too scary, and Rei wouldn't read the book. With Shin being so timid, Rei imagined it'd be even harder for him…

But contrary to his expectations, his baby brother exclaimed with glittering eyes.

"Pickchur book!"

"It says 'happy birthday to you,' Shin."

There were two letters included with the book, one of them a birthday card. It was written in large, easy letters so a child could read it. The other was an envelope addressed to their father, so Rei handed the book and card over to Shin. The book was small enough for Rei to carry with one hand, but too large for Shin's small hands, so he had to hug it with both arms.

The boy gazed with sparkling eyes at the skeleton on the cover—which, again, Rei thought was quite creepy—so Rei asked, with a stiff expression, "…Want me to read it for you?"

"Yeah!"

* * *

The Giadian Empire may have changed in both name and nature to the Giadian Federacy, but the Nouzen clan still had great influence over the military and government. And so, their villa in the capital was so large and vast that the children of the servant families would always get lost during their apprenticeships.

The marquis's office, with a carpet alone large enough to match the size of a civilian home, the Marquis of House Nouzen, Seiei Nouzen, looked to his butler who stood at attention. The butler had black, hawk-like eyes, the pitch-black of a pureblood Onyx.

"Stuart."

"Yes, sir?"

A major noble's servant was to be like his shadow, silent and omnipresent until directly called. He stepped forward, clad in an anachronistic tailcoat and monocle, and Marquis Nouzen looked up at him from his desk.

"You have a grandson who turns eighteen today, if I recall?"

"He's attending the officer's academy. I believe he's much too lacking and it's still too soon for me to introduce him to you, sir."

"I hear he's quite talented, but that's not what I was trying to ask. It's just…"

This brave, old general, who once had half the Imperial army under his command, fell quiet like a neophyte commander who had no idea how to lead soldiers.

"What would you say would be a good present a boy that age would appreciate?"

The old butler smiled in realization.

"You mean for Master Shinei?"

This was the child of Reisha, Marquis Nouzen's firstborn son who eloped to a neighboring country, making Shinei his grandson. Due to the outbreak of the Legion War and the international divide it caused, the boy's survival was unknown for nine years, but the Federacy took him into protection when he was discovered on the battlefield two years ago.

He was currently under the protection of the interim president, and ever since the marquis got word of his survival, he'd been requesting a meeting, but Shin himself refused.

"Well… A gift for an eighteen-year-old boy should probably be…"

The old butler nodded solemnly. "Pocket money."

Marquis Nouzen sank his head to the dignified ebony desk in a show of exasperation. He then raised his head and shouted.

"Something that practical can't possibly be the present his grandfather sends him for his first birthday in recent memory, can it?!"

"You could send it in cash."

"Enough!" Marquis Nouzen shouted at his childhood friend, who brought a hand to his mouth in an attempt to stifle laughter. It seemed half a century wasn't long enough to dull his talents at agitating the marquis!

"Still, you do not know what Master Shinei's tastes are, yes?"

"Well… No, I don't."

"To begin with, once they're over the age of ten, even grandchildren who live in the same home as their grandparents tend to spend more time with their peers than they do with their family. At that point it's hard to know what a child wants, so I suggest giving them money so they may buy whatever they like. And yet, despite never even meeting the boy, you pretend to know what he might like. You don't know your place, pfft…"

"Silence!"

This time Stuart chuckled on purpose. Seeing the marquis grab his head in desperation, the old butler contained his teasing smile.

"…He still does not wish to meet you. I believe Master Shinei is saying he hasn't put his feelings in order yet. You wish to celebrate his birthday while keeping that in mind, yes? In that case, express that desire to celebrate. Send him something that would bless the fact that he has lived thus far. I believe that would be the right idea."

"Oh, and Captain, a package arrived for you while you were dispatched. Take it with you."

"A package?"

Shinei furrowed his brows in confusion when the sergeant in charge of the Rüstkammer base—the Strike Package's home base—told him this. They'd just returned from two months of deployment in the United Kingdom that spring, and it was now early summer.

He didn't remember ordering or asking for any packages in that time period. Since the Eighty-Six lost their families to the Republic's persecution, they had no one to send them letters or packages.

The sergeant regarded Shin's dubious expression with disinterest and walked to the back of the storage room to retrieve the package. To Eighty-Sixers who spent their childhoods on the battlefield, the Federacy's mail order system was a truly curious thing, and apparently quite a few of them placed orders that arrived during their time away in the United Kingdom. Their packages had to take up space in storage while they were away, of course, so the sergeant was very much adamant about them taking them quickly.

"Here you are… There's your receipt, please sign right here."

He shoved a package light enough to be carried in one hand, along with an electronic pen and paper used for receipts.

The package had a stamp on it that indicated it had been opened and resealed by the military for inspection, but upon seeing the name written on both the package's tag and the receipt…

Shin froze up and blinked.

"Marquis Nouzen?"

This was apparently his grandfather, a noble from the former Empire. So far, Shin rejected requests to see him, as well as the possibility of the marquis coming over instead. He never sent Shin letters or packages, though…

"You had your birthday while you were away, right, Captain? It arrived that day. Must be a present. Uh, happy belated birthday."

"Yeah…"

Right, it was his birthday, wasn't it? Shin headed back to his room, thinking that they just barely made it back for Lena's birthday, and used a multi-tool knife to tear the package open. To date, he thought he didn't want see his grandfather; not that he could do without seeing him, but rather that he didn't *want* to.

But now, he didn't think so. It wasn't that Shin particularly wanted to see him now, but he no longer felt like he didn't want to, either.

Shin simply felt that he *should* see him—if he was to come to terms with the things he lost, and the things he longed to recover but dreaded losing.

The box that emerged from the wrapping had a bombastic brand logo and was wrapped in a black silk ribbon that looked like it was weaved out of darkness. Though he felt that it was a bit in bad taste, something about it felt like it touched on some old memory. Shin opened the lid on the box.

"...A picture frame?"

It was a picture frame fashioned like a book—or an album, meant for family use, that could fit multiple pictures. The silver glass pages to contain the images were all empty, except for one that had a card with the familiar image of a skeleton inserted into it.

I was advised that giving this to you again might make you happy. Happy birthday.

"..."

He didn't recognize this handwriting, but for some reason those letters, written with so much graceful flourish that they were a little hard to read, reminded him of something old and distant. Shin traced his fingers over them.

There were no photos of his brother or parents left anymore. Shin couldn't remember any of their faces. But maybe Marquis Nouzen had photos or letters his father sent him. Maybe he could fill this picture frame with memories.

Perhaps this was his way of sending Shin an invitation. Come over to fill it up, to see me. Or perhaps...

Shin smiled without even realizing it. He felt like this old man he never met was pushing him forward.

"Are you telling me to fill it up with the memories I'll find from now on, Marquis Nouzen?"

He couldn't call him "Grandfather" yet. But for now, he could go over and ask for the meaning behind the picture frame, behind the drawing of the skeleton.

With that thought in mind, Shin placed the empty picture frame on his desk.

The Reaper Never Learns

"...Captain Nouzen."

Those words that followed a long silence came across as very clearly and directly...exasperated. Quite unlike the tone of Chief of Staff Willem Ehrenfried, who always seemed to read into people's intentions.

"It seems to me you have some deficiencies in your learning abilities. Don't tell me that you forgot that all Federacy Feldreß, the Reginleif included, have a mission recorder that keeps a log of everything the pilot says."

The chief of staff and all the attending high officers' gazes all fixed on one spot—on Shin, who was seated on a pipe chair brought into the room, frozen like an ice statue.

One of the officers, with the kind of archaic smile usually reserved for grandfathers witnessing the aftermath of a grandchild's prank, operated a nearby holo-window and tapped a play button, playing a part of a rewound audio file.

"Don't leave me behind."

The person on the pipe chair seemed to have spasmed a little, but the chief of staff ignored it.

"Captain Nouzen, I do realize you're only eighteen years old, so some youthful indiscretion is, well, understandable. But while understandable, I must ask that you refrain from doing things like these in the middle of an operation. Surely you understand how this conference felt when we played this recording, yes? Saying it was hard to endure would be a gross understatement."

They were high officials and generals, after all—men who climbed to the top ranks of the army. After a decade of war, the average age in the army became much lower than it was during peacetime, but most of the people in the room were old enough to have children of their own. The only one who was still a bachelor and in his twenties was Willem, a brigadier general.

They all remembered what being Shin's age was like, of course, but they'd since learned to make a clear delineation between that and their duties, and knew to maintain proper appearances. They wouldn't conduct themselves as they did during their younger days, and at their age they very much tried to sweep their memories of such youthful indiscretions under the rug.

Only to then be hit square in the face with a line as youthful and dramatic as that.

Aaah.

It's strange how amazing youth can be, isn't it?

It was a truly surreal moment where the high officials all had faraway looks in their eyes. Grethe, who heard the same recording, couldn't bring herself to prank Shin by playing it in the briefing again, and was downed with her head resting against her desk for a good while.

And the state of the officers in the conference, who had just listened to the recording, was much the same.

"Aha-ha-ha, you really are in the height of youth, aren't you, Captain? Aha-ha-ha-ha!"

"Calm down, get a grip! Don't think back on how Poemy turned you down!"

"Eimi… I miss you, Eimi… I wanna eat your apple pie…"

"Give her a call. And stop sobbing. Trust me, we all want to go home."

"My daughter… My baby girl's going to get snatched away by someone just like this someday… I have to get rid of all the nobodies who might try to take her away…!"

"Getting overprotective is just going to make her hate you, you know. And I'm pretty sure using a 30 mm machine gun against personnel is overkill."

"...As you can see, the damage caused is significant. So please, refrain from doing this ever again. Please."

"He said it twice, that's how important this is."

"Just saying, Willem, but back when you were his age, I wanted to tell you to moderate yourself, too. Really, whenever Grethe was involved, you—"

"Say any more and I may have to tell your wife about your early romances, Richard. Including the love letters you sent."

"?! How do you know about those...?!"

"You never had any talent for writing, so you came to me to put your thoughts on paper. Have you forgotten? And I kept a copy on the side."

"On the side?! I swear, you are such a...!"

"Brigadier General Ehrenfried, Major General Altner, can you take this somewhere else?"

"No, wait. Altner, that's inappropriate. If you pine for a woman, you should use your own words, no matter how crude you are. That's the way of the Imperial noble."

"And you too, Ehrenfried. Writing someone else's love letters for them...? Actually, I didn't know you could write. Color me surprised."

Shin could hear some grumbling coming from elsewhere, with everyone else lying on the table, laughing. Either that, or they were homesick and missing their wives, or had very blank eyes as memories they wished to forget flashed in their minds. The oldest generals took out candy, looking like grandparents hearing about their grandchildren's love affairs. The lieutenant general who commanded the western front's army was holding back laughter, his face twitching.

All of these commanders' dignity had all but evaporated. If the minutes of this meeting were to leak to the public, the army could collapse—which was why there was no record of this meeting to begin with.

And Shin, the sole outsider to witness this shameful affair, was still frozen like an ice statue.

Feeling some pity, the second lieutenant that served as the chief of staff's aide, who sat in the chair diagonally behind him, leaned in and whispered into Shin's ear.

"Captain, I'll show you how to delete the data file in secret later."

"I heard that, Jonas. Don't share illegal information like that in the open… To begin with…" Willem breathed out in shock. "…I doubt the captain even heard you. I think his soul might have slipped away."

Meanwhile, Annette and Dustin…

"Ah no. I'm not coming along," Annette said with a face that seemed to ask why she had to state the obvious.

Lena fell silent for a few minutes. Now that they were back from the expedition to the United Kingdom, Lena pondered how to spend her day off, but when she approached Annette, that was the answer she got.

"Why not?"

"Don't get me wrong, I appreciate the offer. But visiting the president's house is a little too much for me. Too heavy."

"Yeah, same here…," Dustin agreed modestly.

He'd been a member of the first armored group since the Strike Package started in April and was currently on leave. This was also true of Lena, who was operations commander, and Annette, who was a Para-RAID research staff member.

Since Lena and Annette had no homes to go back to following the fall of the Republic, President Ernst Zimmerman—the foster father for Shin's group—invited them to his estate.

Incidentally, she overheard Mr. Zimmerman's phone call with Shin the other day, where they discussed their time off, and he didn't strike her as a very "heavy" person at all. To be more exact, she heard him shout *Then let's have a welcome home party! Yay*, to have Shin hang up in his face.

"…He didn't strike me as a very strict or formal person."

If anything, he seemed quite pleasant. Perhaps to a tiresome degree.

"It's not about his character, it's just his title. He's still president…

Anyway, I just want to take my day off and chill. And there's something I want to work out during my leave."

"Work out?"

"I want to go back to Shin's house in the Republic and look over the library. After Shin's family was taken away, my family bought all the property that wasn't looted from their home and put it in storage... Shin's started seeing his grandparents, right? I figured he might want to see stuff like that, too."

Dustin hummed and turned his eyes to her. "Can I help, Major? If it's a library, I imagine some things there might be too heavy for a girl."

"Mm, I guess. But not anything private. There's a lab there, so I'll handle that alone."

Annette never reported to neither the Republic nor the Federacy that Shin was one of the Espers the Para-RAID technology was based on. She took advantage of the fact that the original documents never mentioned names, and that the trail went cold once the Eighty-Six were taken to the camps.

Even so, Lena cocked her head. Lab notes sounded like they'd be bulky.

"Do you want me to come over and help?"

"How do you figure?" Annette asked with a wry smile. "You just enjoy your time off. You'll be living under the same roof with him, you know?"

Annette didn't specify with whom, but Lena went red just the same. Now that she mentioned it...

"Wait, what? Did you not realize that until now?"

"Yes, hm...," Lena stammered, her face flushed.

Even the usually sincere Dustin sighed with a bit of a frown.

Because You're There (Lena's POV)

And so, Lena was invited to the Federacy's President's—and Shin's group's foster parent's—estate, where she spent the Strike Package's first leave. It was in a quiet neighborhood in Sankt Jeder, a stylish-looking home, but modest considering it was the residence of the man holding power over the largest superpower on the continent.

She went with Theo, Kurena, and Anju, and they were greeted by Frederica, who went home ahead of them; Raiden, who was her chaperone; and Ernst. Shin had returned with Frederica and Raiden, but he was currently at his grandfather's home.

Frederica greeted them with a sullen expression. Raiden explained, with a bit of a sardonic smile, that she had been scolded thoroughly by Ernst and the maid, Theresa, for getting hurt during the Dragon Fang Mountain assault.

Shin called and said he'd be back after having dinner at his grandfather's house, so they had dinner without him before retiring to the living room for a conversation. The fact that all the dishes Theresa cooked were traditional Republic cuisine made Lena tear up a little.

Shin soon returned home, and Frederica—who couldn't raise her dominant arm due to her injury—fawned over him. Ernst lost spectacularly in a card game and became childishly depressed. Before long the sun set and Frederica started nodding off, and so the fun times were put to a temporary close.

The bedroom Lena was given was apparently prepared for her—the bed was set with fabrics in girly colors. Crawling under the covers, sleepiness immediately washed over Lena. As she dozed off, she thought back on that day… It was a fun, blissful day. She wished it could go on forever. Everyone was smiling, even Shin, with how little he emoted.

And then, Lena realized.

The room adjacent to this bedroom. Shin showed her to this room earlier, only to turn on his heels and enter the room next door. And since everyone said they were going to sleep and went to their rooms, that must have been his room.

In other words…

The only thing separating the room she was in now and Shin's bedroom was a single wall.

The moment Lena realized that, she felt her face flush for some reason. With everyone asleep, the room was silent, and that silence made

Lena feel like she could sense something. The presence on the other side of the wall, its breathing, a body warmth slightly higher than her own.

Of course, Lena knew she couldn't possibly have felt any of this, and this was all her imagination. As snug as the president's estate may have been, it wasn't so cheaply built that the walls would be thin enough to hear noises from the adjacent room. Especially not Shin's breathing or presence, given his tendency to not make noises.

However, this might have actually been the first time she spent so much time in close proximity to him...

She cradled her steaming cheeks, wordlessly whispering those words. They'd spent some months in the same base, but they were just a colonel and a captain. Their rooms were in different areas, and their daily schedules didn't mesh at all. They may have had private conversations during meals and free time, but there were always the eyes of onlookers to consider.

But not today. Today was a first. Her first time seeing Shin in casual clothes...and her first time seeing him look so relaxed as he lounged. This was Shin as he looked in a private moment, unlike anything she saw on base or the battlefield. Unfocused, a bit leisurely. He wasn't the eastern front's Headless Reaper, or the commander of the Strike Package—he was just Shin, in his simplest, most unadorned self.

It was a new way of seeing him...and also made her a bit restless. It made the fact that she had walked into a private space, with all duties and positions cleared away—that she'd made it so close to him—abundantly clear, and it made her pulse race.

The sound of her heart throbbing felt oddly loud in the silence of the night. At least, it did to her ears.

Shin can't hear it, can he...?!

The thought made her even more restless, prompting Lena to pull the blanket, from which wafted the fragrance of flowers, over her head.

Because You're There (Shin's POV)

And so, despite having visited his grandfather's dwelling for the first time, Shin turned down the invitation to stay the night and returned to Ernst's, his foster parent's, home. When he opened the front door, he was greeted with a smile by Lena, his friends, and Frederica. It still didn't feel like Ernst's house was home, a place he belonged to, quite yet, but…

Lena's eyes looked a bit teary for some reason. Apparently it was because she was deeply moved by Theresa cooking Republic cuisine.

To Shin, the Republic wasn't a place he saw as his native country or his homeland, but to Lena, it was a home to look back on fondly, a place of memories… It made him come to the—perhaps belated—realization that expecting her to forget or discard it was much more easily said than done. The Strike Package was made up of Eighty-Sixers persecuted by the Republic, so she had to be considerate of their feelings, but…she never got the chance to mourn her homeland's fall. And Shin never noticed. It felt like he was somehow blind to it without even realizing it.

It made him feel like he should absolutely take care to be more attentive to things like that. Like Lena said on the snowy battlefield, to talk to her more. Even if it meant starting from the little things and working their way up.

Frederica's favorite card game was being played on the living room table, and Shin joined the game halfway through. Lena glared at her fan-shaped hand of cards with a focus entirely unlike the way she looked at operation maps, with the carefree expression of a regular girl, and it made Shin crack a smile despite himself. Putting aside how Frederica, who hurt her dominant hand in the previous battle, took advantage of her injury to pester him for attention, the only real fly in the ointment was Ernst's depressed attitude at having thoroughly lost.

Before long, it was nighttime, and Frederica was starting to nod off, and so the fun times were put to a temporary end.

"Good night, then, Shin."

"Yes, good night."

He took Lena to the bedroom Theresa prepared for her and left. He went into his room—he never got used to it, probably because it was markedly more spacious than any room he had in the Eighty-Sixth ward or the army—and slipped into his bed.

And then, the realization set in.

Since Ernst's estate had more rooms than occupants, all the empty rooms were treated as guest rooms. In fact, Shin and his group's rooms were originally guest rooms, and Shin out of all his group was given a room adjacent to an empty one, since that would be the most quiet.

In other words.

The only thing separating his bedroom and the one Lena was staying in now was a single wall.

The moment he realized that, relief washed over him.

...She was right next to him. Close by. She wasn't going to disappear without warning. No one was going to take her away, cruelly, unreasonably. He wasn't going to be left behind.

And that fact was a major relief. That made all the tension drain from his body at once, and he was overcome with an almost forceful sleepiness.

As his consciousness rapidly sank into the quagmire of sleep, her voice as he heard it through the Resonance, like the chiming of a silver bell, came to mind.

I will never leave you behind. I'll always be waiting. I promise.

Because she said those words, he would go on. And then, the words she told him two years ago, when he thought everything was coming to an end.

He felt like now, he could give her a different answer. With that final thought, Shin yielded himself to the darkness of slumber, feeling oddly satisfied.

April 20th (Theo's Birthday)

Giving out birthday presents became something of a trend among the Eighty-Six. Since they'd forgotten their birthdays, they had little conception of celebrating them, but seeing Republic citizens, like Lena, Annette, and Dustin, as well as Federacy citizens, like Grethe and Marcelle, do it made them develop an interest. They'd mostly send little gifts, like sweets and plush toys, to their friends from the same unit and former squad mates.

Or perhaps returning from the United Kingdom and moving to the attached school's dorms during their leave helped ease their tension.

Either way…

"Here you go, Theo. It's a bit belated, but happy birthday."

"No, erm… I know it's become a thing here, but…"

Theo wearily looked down at the "present" Anju handed him with a smile.

"I mean, my birthday's supposed to be in April, you know? And we're in July. You don't have to go out of your way to celebrate it."

Since their birthdays were discovered during the expedition to the Republic, Theo and all the other members with April birthdays couldn't celebrate on time. Still, it did make him a little happy when Lena gave him a set of colored pencils as a belated present before their trip to the United Kingdom.

And the fact that seeing this inspired the others to celebrate birthdays even if they were belated was something he was overall content with… But if they really wanted to celebrate—

"That's just not acceptable. Take it."

"You're totally lying! You and Shin and Raiden and everyone, you're just teasing me!" Theo ended up shouting despite himself.

Anju handed him a cute fox plush, just large enough to sit on the palm of his hand. On its own, it was fine—it wasn't to Theo's taste—but he understood that they were thinking about his Personal Mark.

The problem was that just fifteen minutes ago Shin came over with an apologetic expression and handed him another comical fox present; and fifteen minutes before that Kurena came over; and fifteen minutes before *that* it was Raiden and Annette and Frederica, all of them giving him fox themed accessories and plush toys and fairy-tale books as presents.

After getting so many of the same kind of gift, he had to assume this was all a practical joke.

"Oh, and this is from Shiden. She figured you'd have a hard time carrying all these fox goods."

"...A fox basket? Where do they even sell this stuff?! And Shiden, I can hear you laughing over there!"

Some ten minutes later, Dustin showed up, and—for lack of a better idea—gave him a plush of a racoon that was drawn in a pair with a fox in some country or another, only for Theo to promptly sock him in the face.

"...Ow... This is Sagittarius. Successfully stalled the target... I think he's going to get seriously mad soon. How are things on your end?"

"Snow Witch to Sagittarius. Good work, Dustin. You can head back now," Anju told Dustin, who had taken on the noble role of sacrifice to stall the target.

She spoke to him via the Resonance. While bringing RAID Devices into school grounds was forbidden, today they had special permission. Or rather, they would be given permission after the fact.

"All right. Lena, we're counting on you."

"Yes, here I go!"

As Lena ran off, her long silver hair was speckled with colored dust. Annette sighed as she watched her go.

"I didn't think it would take this long..."

"We wouldn't have made it in time if I didn't come up with stalling tactics, would we?" Shiden laughed out loud.

"...I'm still a bit iffy on that, though...," Shin remarked with narrowed eyes.

The materials they used to stall with were hurriedly collected from the nearby town, with Shin and Lena being sent to get them (everyone decided it should be them since they had walked around town on a tour of the city that doubled as a date and knew the place). Because of that, Shin, too, was quite fed up with having to deal with fox memorabilia.

Raiden spoke, clapping his hands to shake the powder off of them.

"'Sides, using pre-prepared stuff just feels pretty tasteless."

"True."

Kurena looked up at the fruit of their labor proudly and nodded. She rubbed the back of her hand against her nose, unaware that there was a spot of paint on the tip, and smiled while smearing a pink line across her face.

They were in one of the school's empty classrooms. There wasn't a single chair or table in the room, only the teacher's stand and a blackboard—an old-fashioned, deep green blackboard without a single green spot left on it. It had been covered in colors by everyone, save for the few that stepped out to stall their target. It had depleted several sticks of chalk, and everyone was covered in dust before they knew it.

Even so.

"He always draws for us, so this time we should be drawing for him."

Five minutes later, Lena brought a wary Theo over to the classroom, where he froze up with his mouth hanging open. There he found a large trunk containing an art supply set that everyone pitched in to buy. Past the trunk was the blackboard, with everyone's Personal Marks drawn on it, with his in the center.

Star Shower Lemonade

The Eighty-Six, the elites that survived the Eighty-Sixth ward's battlefield of certain death. And yet, what they were in truth were boys and girls in their teens, with all the overactive curiosity and recklessness that entailed.

"I swear. What are you doing…?" Lena grumbled.

Her hair and clothes were drenched, the fragrance of lemon hung over her, and her skin prickled from the carbonic acid.

Apparently, when you introduced a certain type of candy to carbonated drinks, it would foam and burst out violently. When Shin and the other senior Eighty-Six heard about it (who in the world even told them?), they had to try it out.

And to make things worse, a single 500 ml bottle would have surely been enough to experiment, but all ten of them had to do it with a 2-liter bottle each, all at the same time. The result was as disastrous as one would expect; over 20 liters worth of lemonade shot to a surprising height of two meters, producing pillars of foamy liquid that doused everyone in the vicinity, including Lena, who happened to be walking by.

The Eighty-Six were boys and girls in their teens, with all the over-active curiosity and recklessness that entailed, including the occasional impulsiveness that resulted in a major screwup.

Shiden, Raiden, Theo, Claude, Tohru, and Yuuto instantly fled upon seeing Lena get caught in the splash zone, leaving Shin all alone. He was frozen in place, his expression fixed in an expression that screamed *Dammit.*

He then dropped his shoulders. "…Sorry."

"Geez…"

His face looked so dejected it drained Lena of any will to get angry. The thick fragrance of lemon still clung to her, and her skin still prick-led from carbonic acid popping atop it. For some reason, the thought crossed her mind that it was like the sparkling of stars in the galaxy.

"I'll let you off the hook this time because it's summer, and you did it outdoors. But be careful next time."

She looked up at the troublemaker, who stood slightly taller than her despite being her age, and cracked a bit of a smile. It was like she was his scolding big sister.

July 12th (Lena's Birthday)

"Happy birthday, Lena," said Raiden as he shoved a large tote bag made from sailcloth into Lena's hands. It was a faint pink color and had a cat embroidered onto it. Its design was cute, but its wide gusset and the strong fabric so emphasized utility that it felt less like a present and more like a housewife's shopping bag.

"Thank you. That's today, come to think of it…"

She was so busy it slipped her mind.

"Yeah... Anyway, good luck today."

...At what?

It soon became clear why Raiden picked such a large shopping bag for her.

"Oh, there you are, Lena. Happy birthday. Here."

When she ran into Theo in the hall, Theo handed her a book of scenery paintings adorned with a ribbon.

"Y-you gave me a present that one time, so this is just me returning the favor. That's all, okay?"

Kurena averted her flushed face as she handed Lena a picture frame with a decoration of a cute cat on it.

"It smells nice, so put it on your desk, if you'd like... Just be sure to clean up your desk, so you don't end up with a pile of documents that'll hide it, okay?"

With an impish smile, Anju handed Lena a potpourri of roses packed in a heart-shaped basket.

"Accept this, if you will. It should make a good snack with tea."

Frederica gave her violet flowers preserved in sugar, packed in what looked like a jewelry box.

"Here you go, Lena, from me. Put it on if there's a party or something."

Annette gave her a small choker inlaid with red and silver jewels and fashioned like an orange flower.

"Happy birthday, Colonel. How about you try this for a change?"

Grethe gave her a tube of wine-red lipstick with a very vivid brand logo on it.

* * *

"Oh, Colonel, I know you look out for me a lot, so take this as a gift from your subordinate."

With his eyes darting around like he was wary a certain someone might be watching, Dustin gave her a handkerchief set.

"Your Majesty, Your Majesty! I know a certain someone hasn't sent you this yet, so make sure to put it on."

Shiden gave Lena a cloisonné ring while wearing a very wide smirk on her lips.

"Colonel Milizé, I hear it's your birthday."

"This is from us, then. Plants that produce tea are limited in the Federacy, so finding a shop that deals in tea leaves was a challenge."

For some reason, Major General Altner and Chief of Staff Willem, who happened to be in Rüstkammer base, gifted her a can of synthesized tea and a porcelain tea set.

"*Pi!*"

Even Fido gifted her an out-of-season branch of *lilas* flowers it found in the nearby woods.

It seemed like someone called her over every few steps, each of them blessing her birthday in their own way and giving her more and more presents. Lena didn't expect to have her birthday celebrated like this, giving her a bit of a ticklish but happy feeling nonetheless.

The largely built head cook walked by her and said, "Colonel, today we're serving a birthday menu for all the people who have their birthdays in July!" with a hearty grin. And eventually, she was able to tow her now full and quite heavy tote bag back to her office.

Huh?

Or so she thought, but her adjutant, Second Lieutenant Isabella Perschmann, was waiting for her in an unusual place, right in front of the lounge suite. Her slender form hid the silver-lipped low table from sight.

Standing still in her strange position, Second Lieutenant Perschmann spoke with her usual detached tone.

"The bouquet is from me."

"Ah… Thank you."

Was that why she was standing in this spot?

"It's very delicate, though it might be a bit heavy for a lady, so I can understand bringing it over. I'd have preferred if he waited, though."

"…?"

Second Lieutenant Perschmann ignored Lena's puzzled look, picked up the *lilas* flowers Fido gave Lena, set them in a vase behind her, and walked out. With this, Lena could finally see the low table. A crystal vase sat there, adorned with a bouquet of lilies and the *lilas* branch.

And sitting in the shadow of the flowers was something else that wasn't there when Lena left the office this morning.

A box with a foreign-looking design, made of rosewood and sprinkled with silver dust and mother-of-pearl, with a diagonal tube extending from one side of it—allowing one to peer inside—and a circular mirror at the base. In simple terms, it looked like a microscope.

There was a largish screw attached to the box, reminiscent of a music box. Turning it made it play a melody Lena didn't know, but one that felt strangely familiar. At the lower part of the tube, crumbs of precious stones revolved inside the glass mirror to the rhythm of the melody. The mirror attached to the cylinder was apparently a kaleidoscope, reflecting a multi-colored pattern reminiscent of a peacock's tail or a rose window.

It was…pretty.

She looked at it, entranced, without even realizing. By the tune that invoked a sense of nostalgia, and the dancing, shifting, colored lights.

She held her breath for a moment, losing track of time, and knew somehow that this was why the one who sent it chose this present. Under the box's four collapsible legs was a note with the Federacy's symbol of the double-headed eagle. On it was a single line of text, scribbled with familiar, handsome handwriting.

Happy birthday, Lena.

Lena couldn't help but giggle. As tactical commander, he was busy with all sorts of tasks. She knew that he was held up in the hangar today with the maintenance and research teams testing a Reginleif system update. And still…

"Really, you could have waited…Shin."

She said this, blind to the fact that she herself ran away from him on his birthday in May.

May 19th (Shin's Birthday), a Little Trick

"Captain Nouzen."

Turning around, Shin found himself facing a girl wearing the Republic's Prussian blue uniform without putting her hands through its sleeves, who had white, silvery hair. It was Major Henrietta Penrose, affiliated with the Eighty-Sixth Strike Package's technological department.

"Yes, Major Penrose?"

"You can just call me Annette. I don't like all these titles."

For some time after first meeting him, Annette always looked like she was on the cusp of saying something. Now she looked oddly candid, like she'd forgotten about all that. Shin carried the philosophy book that had just been returned to him after he'd misplaced it the other day, and Annette glanced at the silver bookmark inserted into it before going on.

"I heard it's your birthday this month. I know I caused you some trouble, so take this as an apology."

She thrust out her hand, holding out a case of cuff links. It was an accessory meant to hold together a shirt's sleeves, except it was mostly used for full dress, making it something one would rarely use. Certainly they wouldn't be worn with a military uniform or battle dress, but not even in service dress.

"...Are you asking me to accept this?"

"I just said it was as an apology."

"But I don't think I have a use for them."

"I'd have even less of a use for them if you gave them back. But you're still an officer, so if there's ever a party, you can use it when you dress up for that."

Even if such a chance happened upon him, he wouldn't go. That thought seemed to show on his face, because Annette heaved an exasperated sigh.

"If there's a party, attend it. And put these on when you do... Got it?"

She pushed the box into his hands, leaving no room for argument. The cuff links were inlaid with small red and silver jewels, designed like a delicate orange flower. Anette then pointed a willowy finger at his face with a bit of a sulking expression.

"Especially considering you might end up escorting Lena in the future, you have to wear these."

In Annette's room was the matching choker she ordered in a set with these cuff links, which she would gift Lena on her birthday two months later. But of course, Shin had no way of knowing that.

July 12th (Lena's Birthday) – Part 2

"Milizé."

Lena turned around, finding herself faced with Vika and Lerche standing behind him. He was dressed in the United Kingdom's summer uniform with the Strike Package's Lieutenant Colonel rank insignia.

It was past the Rüstkammer base's working hours and almost dinnertime, and Lena was in the first barracks, where she lived and worked. The corridor was quite deserted at this time of day, with the rays of tired sunlight preceding a late summer dusk shining faintly through the colored glass window panes. The chirping of birds could be heard in the distance.

"I realize it's belated, but happy birthday… My apologies. I would have liked to celebrate with you, but if I were to send you a personal present, things could be tricky."

Lena was taken aback by the statement for a moment, but then understood and nodded with a smile. Vika was royalty, and any gift he gave her or the Eighty-Six would be seen as a bestowal or medal—in other words, it would carry political significance.

"It's all right, it's the thought that counts…" Recalling something, she then added in an impish manner. "You already gave me that lovely dress."

Sending a woman a dress was a gesture made by a parent, a lover, or a spouse. Vika simply shrugged off the implication in an exaggerated but elegant manner.

"That wasn't a gift from me, but from the royal family, since you were our invited guest… Looking back on it, I really put my life on the line when I gave you that dress, didn't I?"

Lena looked at him quizzically as he uttered this strange comment to himself, and he waved it away.

"Either way… To make up for that—"

His emperor-violet eyes flickered for a second, going from Lena to another direction—the corridor connecting the barracks to its adjacent hangar.

"—I closed off the hangar's connecting corridor."

"Lady Zashya scattered documents all over the place prior to this," Lerche appended, standing a step behind Vika.

"…Erm." Lena blinked, unsure as to what to make of the comment.

"Knowing him, he wouldn't stand there and wait for her to finish, since that would make him feel like he's rushing her, so he'd likely take a detour."

"And since those documents contain confidential information, Lady Zashya would say she doesn't need help picking them up, so it's unlikely he would help her."

And so, Vika spoke as he prepared to walk away. He glanced at a usually unused passage in the deserted hallway to Lena's side, where the chirping birdsong was coming from.

"Wait here for a bit… He should be coming soon."

After hearing this much, even Lena guessed who he was talking about.

An unused passage in the back of the deserted barracks. It made for quite a detour from the dining hall and the hangar, so people rarely walked through this passage. From the other side, she saw a person's shadow cast over the golden sunlight shining through greenery. The moment she spotted him, she ran over.

"…Shin!"

At the end of the tunnel paved with fallen leaves from the elm trees planted along the roadside was Shin, who had come from the hangar. He blinked upon seeing Lena hurry over.

"Lena… You were waiting for me here?"

"Yes. I haven't had a chance to thank you for the birthday present, after all."

The two of them, all alone in an empty, private space. This is why Vika had been acting the way he did. To begin with, Shin was busy all day with a strain test for a Juggernaut system update. It ended up lasting longer than expected, leaving Shin occupied in the hangar until nearly lights-out. Right now, he stepped out for a bit to have dinner, and once he was done eating he was to return to the hangar, which would leave Lena no time to thank him for the birthday present.

Shin furrowed his brows ever so slightly, confused.

"I thought you were busy, too, so I thought it'd be fine that way… You gave me a present on my birthday, too, after all."

Saying this, Shin then shook his head. That wasn't it—a denial directed more at himself than at Lena.

"I sent you that present because I wanted to. You always work yourself to the bone, and I thought you might like it."

Hearing this, a smile bloomed on Lena's face.

"Yes. And I wanted to thank you for it."

A fancy, meticulously made music box, with a kaleidoscope attached, built specifically to simulate one's senses of sight and sound alike. A curio like that surely wasn't sold at any corner; he must have spent a lot of time looking and picking one out.

"Thank you… I love it, and I promise I'll cherish it."

Hearing this, Shin regarded her with a smile. "I'm glad you want to cherish it, but don't just treat it as an ornament. Put it to use, just like I use the bookmark."

"Yes, of course."

The transiently shifting, beautiful shades of light, and a crisp tune plucked by metal. A melody that beckoned feelings of nostalgia. Listening to it, she'd no doubt experience the same dream every night.

A dream of blue mechanical butterflies fluttering across the blue expanse, and a field of red crimson lycoris flowers spanning as far as the eye can see. And there would stand the boy she hadn't met face-to-face yet but was able to reunite with.

"Are you going to dinner after this, Shin?"

"Yes… The tests are taking longer than expected, so once I'm done eating, I'll be heading back."

So, it was like she thought.

"That sounds rough. But apparently the head cook really put a lot of effort into today's dinner," Lena said, naturally taking his hand and pulling him by the arm.

And with her bright, carefree smile, like the blooming of an elegant silver flower…

"I think you're allowed to at least enjoy your dinner."

Mornings started early in the army, and it was still dark out the window as Lena got dressed in her room.

Her room was more full of things since yesterday, and the black cat

TP curiously looked around, exploring the new discoveries scattered about. She'd trained him to not get on desks and shelves, so he only looked at the presents, but his large eyes sparkled just the same.

A few gifts were sitting on her small, personal desk. A picture stand holding a picture of a badly focused, poor-quality photo that made it hard to tell who the people in the picture were. Rose potpourri. A collection of scenery paintings, opened down in the middle. And next to the desk, leaned against the wall, was a sailcloth tote bag stuffed with several plush toys.

Spotting the specially made foreign music box on the corner of her desk, Lena smiled. Facing a large, full-length mirror, Lena fixed her military cap a little. Good. She curled her lips up into a natural smile, turned around with a clicking of her heels and walked out of the room with a spring in her step.

As the door closed, Lena's room remained empty. Sitting atop the small desk in her bedroom, next to the music box, was a diary set on its ends and stuck into it was a silver bookmark. It had a pattern of a red licorice and a Juggernaut—when she had Shin's bookmark ordered, she secretly made herself a matching copy.

As the sun finally rose, a refreshing summer morning began. The shadows cast by the music box and the metallic bookmark standing side by side overlapped, with nowhere there to see it.

Little Shin and Little Annette, to Current Shin and Current Annette

"Shin! Here, happy Valentine's Day!"

His childhood friend from the house next door cheerfully handed him a small package. Shin, who would turn five this year, gazed at the package with a chill running down his back. The pink and red glassine packaging looked cute and innocuous enough, and yet…

Standing right in front of him was his childhood friend Rita—

Henrietta—grinning at him while completely unaware of the thoughts going through his head.

"Erm...," Shin asked gingerly. "Did you make it, Rita...?"

"Yeah...! Ah, don't worry, though! I picked one that didn't make Papa pass out!"

"..."

Shin felt (but knew better than to say aloud) that Rita's father was always in a really poor position.

Whenever little Rita made sweets, her father, Josef von Penrose, always had to taste test them—which was essentially a noble sacrifice—only to fall every time after attempting to eat a few sweets. Just the fact that she made that many attempts was bad news on its own, but that was something Shin, at five years old, couldn't intuit on his own.

"Come on, open it and look!"

"...All right."

He obediently opened the rustling package, which revealed what looked to be cookies. Shin studied them for one silent moment. What is this?

"Heh-heh. Can you guess who it is?"

"..."

Shin tried to think about what she meant. He thought about it *really* hard. *Really, really* hard. And finally, he came up with an answer.

"...A giant monster."

"It's you, Shin! From the class trip this year! I made a cookie that looks like you!"

"..."

It looked a bit too charred to be a cookie and, if this was supposed to be him, he wasn't sure why the batter was warped into the shape of a spider web, making it look nothing like a person's face (this was the result of the cookie refusing to leave the mold, forcing Rita to pull it out). Also, he wasn't sure why he had six or seven eyes.

Do you hate me or something, Rita? Shin nearly asked, but stopped himself. Rita wasn't doing this to be mean. She was just clumsy. Really, really clumsy.

What to do with this, though…? Would Fido eat these cookies? He'd feel bad about letting Fido eat them, to say nothing about how it would be rude to Rita. As he gazed at the cookies (?), Shin was more conflicted than he'd ever been before.

"Hm, Shin… I mean, Captain Nouzen."

As his once childhood friend and current colleague approached him, all smiles, Shin—who had just turned eighteen two months ago—became oddly alert. His experience and intuition, fostered through seven years on a battlefield of certain death, were kicking up alarm bells in his head. He didn't know what it was, but something was wrong. Very, very wrong.

"…Yes, Major Penrose?"

"Oh, what's with the stiff attitude? You've already called me Rita a few times, you can call me that even when we're on base. Anyway, Captain."

Shin had to wonder why she referred to him by his rank after saying all that. A major outranked a captain, which applied an unspoken pressure to obey orders.

Rita—Henrietta, or otherwise Annette—took something out of her lab coat pocket with a smirk.

A red and pink glassine package that looked…or rather, at least *looked* cute and harmless enough. But it was all too close to a nightmare sitting deep within his memories.

"The same portrait cookie I made for you, and the one you called a monster. To celebrate your confession… Or, well, I guess the outcome being what it was, you might not want to celebrate, but I figure I'd give it another try to commemorate it. I think I recreated it perfectly, if I do say so myself… By the way…" Annette flashed a devilish smile. "…I never taste tested it."

"…"

And she said she recreated it…perfectly. Which means that the minimal bit of protection Mr. Penrose once granted him was gone, making it much more dangerous… Shuddering in fear, Shin looked down at the package. Annette, on the other hand, had her lips curled up, like a cat toying with prey.

"You'll take it, right, Shin? I mean, you did steal my best friend away."

October 2nd (Anju's Birthday)

"Happy birthday, Anju. Your birthday is October 2nd, so happy birthday."

With the supply line rationing radically fallen back, she had no idea how he possibly got it, but Anju could only direct a strained smile at Dustin, who held a large bouquet of flowers with a very serious expression.

The bouquet Dustin hid away was one thing, but his overwhelmed, stiff expression and his words stressing that this was her birthday. All of them…

"Thank you. But you don't have to let it bother you, Dustin. I really don't care much about it."

She nodded as he looked back at her. True to her words, she didn't care, and spoke with a gentle smile.

"The fact that the second large-scale offensive happened on my birthday doesn't matter."

Late into the night of October 1st, the satellite bombardment began—and the second large-scale offensive ended on October 2nd, on Anju's birthday.

Apparently, Shin, Lena, Frederica, and Dustin all planned to celebrate her birthday, but they were called back to base due to the second large-scale offensive, and even a day later, Shin, Lena, and the rest of the Strike Package were all swamped with work. As chaos continued on the front lines, they needed to confirm the situation and plan for their next operation.

And yet, piled up behind Dustin was a mountain of presents from everyone. It wasn't simply that everyone entrusted their presents with Dustin out of convenience—they all acknowledged that he had the right to celebrate this day with Anju and shifted the schedule to give them time to do so.

Her comrades from the Eighty-Sixth ward, who survived the battlefield alongside her, acknowledged Dustin. They all blessed the day she came into this world, and they wouldn't let a Legion attack on the same day tarnish that.

Dustin's argent eyes softened with relief and affection.

"...Is that right?"

"Yes, that's right."

Everyone, and you, celebrate this day, after all.

Anju accepted the bouquet he held out to her. It was big, a bundle of flowers in assorted colors. It was like he gathered flowers from any florist he could find, not caring to arrange the flowers or match their aromas. But that, in turn, made them seem more vivid and throbbing with life.

"What's this?"

"Well, I actually ordered a proper bouquet from a florist, but I couldn't pick it up on time, and the flower shop's people had to evacuate. So they gathered all the flowers they had left and came all the way to base, hoping I could use them... About the colors, it was my first time doing this, so I couldn't put them together right..."

"It's pretty enough as it is... I mean it," she appended with an impish smile, seeing his doubtful look.

She honestly thought the bouquet had an awkward sort of beauty to it that fit Dustin's overly serious nature. She hugged the bouquet that looked like a bundle of wildflowers, taking in its strong, suffocating scent.

The Strike Package was preparing for its next operation—it wouldn't be long before the two of them would set out for their next battlefield again. And so...

"I'll take them and turn them into dried flowers."

Since they were setting out to the battlefield, they wouldn't be there to see these flowers spoil—and so, *she wouldn't let these flowers fall.* She would retain their colors and aromas for as long as possible, so that when they returned from battle, they would be there to greet her, unchanged.

So the emotions those flowers contained would always be there to encourage her.

"They'll be ready by the time we come back—and next time, together, let's make another bouquet."

November 12th (Annette's Birthday)

"Theo, I'm sorry. We really need you to do this."

"Sorry, Theo. Could you help us out??"

...And so, Lena—whom he could tell was stumped even through the Para-RAID—and Shin—whom he surmised from their long acquaintance was also troubled—both asked him.

"They said, 'happy birthday, Annette.'"

Upon hearing a knock on the door and opening it with an indifferent "Yes?", Annette found herself faced with a wrapped box with that statement and blinked in surprise.

She had to leave the Strike Package's home base at Rüstkammer base for business and was temporarily staying at a base's lodging house in Sankt Jeder. An Eighty-Six boy with distinctive Jade eyes she ran into often handed her the box and looked at her surprised expression with interest.

"It's from Shin and Lena. They wanted to give it to you personally, but you're here in the capital and those two can't leave their stations, so they asked me to do it."

The Strike Package was currently deployed in the northern second front, with Annette recovering at a sanatorium. What's more, with the second large-scale offensive having happened only a month ago, the transport lines between the front lines and the home front were crowded and in a state of chaos.

With this, the accessory set Lena and Shin ordered for her from a jeweler in Sankt Jeder couldn't be delivered from Rüstkammer base, with the alternate delivery address being their home base. As a result, they had no recourse but to turn to Theo, who left the front lines with an injury and was stationed in Sankt Jeder, where the jeweler was.

"They couldn't get you the right message cards, though. Sorry. They'll send that to you in the mail later. And as for Shiden and the rest, sending packages isn't an option right now, so they'll get you your present when you get back to base."

"Uh, yeah. I figured that much, so it's okay. Thanks."

As stated, the chaos following the second large-scale offensive left the supply lines overcapacity, leaving no place for personal letters or packages, even just a few message cards. Annette knew this and had no intention of saying it bothered or hurt her.

But aside from all that—

"...Why are there three boxes?"

There were two small boxes with matching logos from the same jeweler and another larger box with different wrapping. Seeing Annette's baffled expression, Theo frowned.

"Whaddaya mean, why? I can't just walk up and give you their presents empty-handed, right? Plus, you gave me that fox fairy-tale book, too."

So it was a birthday present from him. Theo's eyes darted around uncomfortably, like he was ill at ease.

"But, fair warning, don't expect much. I don't have the first clue what girls like, and I figured sending you a decoration or something would get in the way when you headed back to base, so I narrowed it down to something you could use on the spot. So, erm..."

He gestured with his hand for her to open the box, so she tore off the neat wrapping and opened it.

What sat inside was—

"Sorry, I basically got you a daily necessity... I just figured you probably don't have your usual cup with you, so I thought you could use it here, at least."

It was a pair of round mugs, their shape reminiscent of an egg, and dyed pretty pastel colors. One was a sky teal, and the other was a faint yellow—it was like they traced the colors of the spring that awaits past the coming winter.

He got them hoping it wouldn't be a gift that would weigh her down; a gift he put thought into in an attempt to get her something she'd need. The feeling behind it made her happy.

"Thanks… Say, why don't I put these to good use right now?"

Theo blinked. "I mean, I gave them to you, so I don't mind."

"Come in, then. I happen to have some cake, even if it is the cheap stuff from the food court's coffee shop. I'll make you some coffee, so have some."

"Huh?"

Since the business that brought her to this base was by no means pleasant, she decided to get herself a snack to keep her mind off things. She got cookies and donuts, too.

The offer made Theo tense up. Seeing him waver in the face of going into a woman's room, Annette laughed.

"I mean, you delivered presents from my friends and got me one yourself. Might as well accept the invitation and have some birthday cake, too, right?"

86

ALL-STAR PERFUME BATTLE

They spent their adolescence there, on the battlefield.

EIGHTY-SIX

Life, land, and legacy.

All reduced to a number.

86 ALTER VOLUME ONE

86

[EIGHTY-SIX]

ALL-STAR PERFUME BATTLE

The pistol being thrust at him was the Republic military's standard issue largish automatic pistol. Its 845 g of weight didn't register as heavy to Shin's hands, but having her dainty fingers grip it looked incredibly cruel, for some reason.

She spoke with those one-of-a-kind argent eyes fixed at him over the gun's coldly glinting sights.

"You and me, facing each other like this. It must have been our fate."

Her voice was chilling. And with half his body covered in red, Shin gazed into her icy eyes.

"Lena..." He called her name softly...

...and then his eyes narrowed in exasperation.

"I get that this whole exercise is over the top, but you don't have to put up this weird act."

†

"Ahem. We'll now begin the all-star battle conducted by the Eighty-Sixth Strike Package and others. This commentary is brought to you by Yatrai Nouzen, with the 10-8 number tag. As for what the number tags mean, you'll understand later. Good luck."

The black-haired young man sitting in the commentator seat, Yatrai, spoke into the microphone in his hands, reading off of a script with a distinct lack of enthusiasm. He lacked all motivation from the get-go, showing that he'd pretty much given up on maintaining his usual dignified facade as a child of the Nouzen clan.

"The participants in this mock battle will be divided into four teams. Each team will correspond to a perfume that is based on, or at least likely to be based on, its main theme ingredient. For example, if the main ingredient of my perfume was ambergris, the sperm Leviathan's fragrance would belong to Team Sparkles… Wait, why call it 'Sparkles'?"

"Ah, yes. I, Joschka Maika, with tag 2-24, will explain the rules. My perfume is champac, which uses flowers for a base, meaning it was used by Team Flower. Of course, as the one in charge of the rules, I won't be participating in the mock battle."

Standing in front of Joschka were the usual members, like Shin and Lena, along with the Eighty-Sixth ward members like, Daiya and Kaie, as well as the Legion team, like Rei and Kiriya. The grown-up team was made up of people like Grethe, Richard, and Willem; the other unit team was made up of Gilwiese and Lieutenant Colonel Mialona; the foreign army team included Ishmael and Hilnå; and the parent team included Václav and Reisha.

In other words, all the named characters in *86—Eighty-Six* were participating. This will list all the fragrances of perfumes each character might use, so feel free to use this as a reference when looking for perfume with the image of your favorite character. The same fragrance can produce different impressions based on how it's mixed, so experiment to find the one you want!

"As previously announced, the teams are decided by which ingredient they're using as well as which part of the ingredient they'll be using. The Flower team will be using flowers as their main ingredient; the Fruit team will be using fruit and seeds; the Leaf team will be using leaves, branches, stalks, and roots; while the Sparkles team will be using saps and resins."

"Why are all the names so dreary…?"

"That last name feels especially malicious..."

Lena and Shin whispered at the front of the group, but Joschka ignored them.

"So the ones using the entirety of grasses, flowers included, go to the Leaf team. Animal extracts, like civet, ambergris, and beeswax, go to the Sparkles team. Resins and animal extracts are rarer, so they get lumped together."

"...If that's how it's divided, doesn't that mean the Flower team holds a supermajority?" Raiden frowned, but once again, Joschka seemed to pay him no mind.

Incidentally, the Flower team also happened to have the most people, while the Sparkles team was half the size.

"Also, for people who use synthesized perfumes that don't exist in nature, we put them in teams that would recreate them. So for ingredients that would be recreated with flowers, we put them in the Flower team, if it's fruit we put them in the Fruit team. Aquanaut is an exception that fits into this, too, so I included them into the fruit group out of personal prejudice."

"Wait, but aquanaut is the fragrance of the sea, right? Why fruit?" Theo pondered, well aware that his question would likely go ignored.

Each person was only informed of what team they belonged to, and so no one knew which team anyone else ended up in. Many of the participants also knew very little about perfumes, and even less about what materials were used in making them. In Theo's case, he had never used an aquanaut perfume and couldn't tell what it smelled like.

"I just figured that's the closest fit, based on my personal impression. I think you'll understand if you run into Mr. Aquanaut, but young Aqua kinda smells like fruit."

"So that's how you decided."

Plus, who's young Aqua?

"And I'm sure right now, everyone but little Aqua wondered 'who's this wittle Aqua...?' In other words, none of you know what perfumes everyone else uses. You won't know who's in your team until you run into them… So, with that in mind, let's explain the mock battle's rules!"

The Rules

- The urban maneuvering grounds will be the designated battlefield. The participants will be placed in different spots at random.
- If you encounter a member of another team, combat will ensue. If both sides do not open fire on each other within a minute of encountering the enemy, both will be disqualified.
- You must distinguish between members of your team and other teams by their perfume.
- If you are hit by members of another team, you are disqualified.
- If you fire at members of your own team, you are disqualified.
- Through verbal exchanges and agreements, it is possible to cooperate with members of your own team.
- Once the number of surviving members for three teams is reduced to zero, the remaining team will be crowned the winner.

"Oh, that's not fair!"

"You said you'd explain the rules, but you let the narrator do it for you…!"

"So put simply, you have to shoot at the enemy, you lose if you get shot, and you also lose if you shoot an ally, and the only way to tell if someone's on your team or not is through their smell."

Once again ignoring Kurena's and Anju's grumbling, Joschka summed up the rules. Having to explain all that in dialogue would bump up the line count, so I just summed it up like this. Bullet points are powerful.

"If you're on Team Flower, people with floral fragrances are on your side. If you're on Team Fruit, people with fruit or seed fragrances are on your side. If you're on Team Leaf, leaf-based fragrances are on your side. And Team Sparkles… Well, I think people who use those kinds of scents will just know. They'll smell like you. And needless to say, there are no IFF devices. So," Joschka said with a smirk. "Well… Good luck out there."

* * *

Kaie suddenly raised her hand. They did say they'd explain it later, after all, and it still wasn't addressed.

"By the way, what's with the numbers on our shirts? Is it, like, what team they're in and what number they're in?"

The numbers on their shirts were evenly color coded into red, green, blue, and yellow. But despite both having the number 1 on their tags, Yuuto and Claude had different colors. Shin's color started with 5, while others had 6, 7, or 8.

"Yes, they're based on the wearer's birthday," Joschka replied indifferently. "People usually distinguish between teams by name tags, so I figured it'd be funny if some people got confused by the numbers. The colors of the tags are also completely random and have nothing to do with your team allotments for the same reason."

Kaie's mouth fell open.

"That's vicious..."

"Crown Prince Zafar, thank you for joining me for commentary. How do you feel about this exercise so far?"

With the rundown of the rules finally finished, the participants moved into the maneuvering grounds and Yatrai turned to the commentators from the reporter's seat. The crown prince of the Republic of Roa Gracia replied with an elegant nod.

"Hm... Are you asking me to introduce my perfume and tag number? I'm Vika's brother, Zafar Idinarohk, tag number 4-29, and my perfume of choice is angelica root... I won't go into the particular type of fragrance, so those curious are welcome to look into it on their own."

"Absolving yourself of that part of the responsibility right away...?"

"I would say that the responsibility to explain it was dropped on me without warning to begin with, so I feel no qualms about shrugging it off... Now, personally speaking, I look forward to seeing my brother put up a good fight, but…" Zafar paused, furrowing his fair brows. "…to begin with, will this even be a normal mock battle?"

Needless to say, it wouldn't.

Only a perfume maker would be able to accurately tell if a perfume was based on flowers, fruit, grass, or sap. How far scent travels and what direction it travels from all depends on the way the wind blows. And lastly, the paint balls they used for the mock battle had a thick smell that got in the way of identifying the perfumes. And indeed…

"Saiki, what the hell? That refreshing scent of yours is spearmint, isn't it?! That means you're on my side!"

"Wait! Captain Eijyu, back off! I can't tell without smelling you! I can't tell if you're on my side… I said back off!"

"Whoa, the way you're running away is pretty insulting! And how are you supposed to smell me if I stay away?! Listen, my color is sage grass, an herb, just like you! We're both Team Leaf… Ah."

"Ah, Second Lieutenant Kukumila."

The way the wind blew made it hard to tell who was on which side, making things confusing, which got Saiki (spearmint, Team Leaf, tag 4-9) and Eijyu (sage, Team Leaf, tag 10-13) easily sniped and taken out by Kurena (blackberry, Team Fruit, 5-6).

"What the hell, Tohru? Aren't you Team Leaf…?! You smell like greenery, so why did you shoot me…?!"

"Yay, you fell for it, Claude! My perfume is galbanum, and while it smells like leaves, but I'm in Team Sparkles! it's made from sap, apparently. Is that your perfume though, Claude? It smells kinda foresty, so I'm guessing you're Team Leaf after all?"

"It's called artemisia—wormwood! Like you said, it's just Team Leaf, plain and simple, dammit!"

Claude (wormwood/artemisia, Team Leaf, tag 1-29) bitterly failed to distinguish friend from foe due to a case of misleading smell and was ruthlessly taken out by Tohru (galbanum, Team Sparkles, 2-14).

"Yay, I did it! I spectacularly took down that annoying Onyx general! "

"Mhm. That was some fancy shooting, I'll admit."

On the other hand, one little girl, Svenja (ylang-ylang, Team Flower, 3-27) was able to identify one case of a strong flowery fragrance even from afar, and took Richard out (vetiver, Team Leaf, tag 12-12). She hopped about happily, the small snub-nosed revolver she carried for self-defense in her hands.

"Stop right there, Shinei's older brother!"

"Give it up, Rei! We know you're (probably) on Team Flower! You ran out of luck when you ran into us!"

"Wait, you two! That's not fair, you're rose and violet, of course you'd know you're on the same team!"

With the two of them having floral scents easy to recognize, Frederica (Damask rose, Team Flower, tag 2-7) and Lena (violet, of course, Team Flower, 7-12) teamed up and were frantically pursuing Rei (styrax, Team Sparkles, tag 10-18).

"I'm surprised you figured out I'm not on Team Flower, Mina!"

"Mm, I couldn't really tell the smell apart, but I figured someone like you would never use floral perfume, Kino."

"That's how you figured it out?!"

With a perfume that smelled similar to flowers, Kino (palmarosa, Team Leaf, tag 9-1) was easily exposed as an enemy by Mina (chamomile, Flower, 12-25), owing to their long acquaintance.

At the same time, President Ernst (basil, Leaf, 4-30) was being persistently pursued by the maid, Theresa, (heliotrope, Team Leaf, 5-30), much to the dismay of the commentators Yatrai, Joschka, and Zafar.

Cases where even smelling the perfume directly made it hard to tell which team they were on made things especially tricky.

"Based on that scent, you're on Team Flower, just like me, Shana. Let's team up."

"Take that!"

"Huh?!"

Feeling a shot to her back, Anju (water lily/lotus, Team Flower, tag 10-2) turned around in surprise, only to find Shana (orris root, tag 11-9) smirking at her impishly.

"Sorry, orris is a type of root, so despite how it smells, I'm Team Leaf," she explained conveniently.

"Huh?! But why?! Michihi, that's apricot perfume, so you're Team Fruit, same as me!" Rito (grapefruit, Team Fruit, 1-5) exclaimed, covered in yellow paint.

"…? My perfume is Osmanthus, that's Team Flower," Michihi (Osmanthus, Team Flower, tag 3-4) said, "You're clearly on another team, Rito."

"Heh-heh… So you fell for it because it smells like citrus perfume just like yours, First Lieutenant Siri. But melissa is made from lemon balm, which isn't actually a citrus fruit at all!"

"Kuh... You're right, and I fell for it… Really, getting fooled by an act like this really is frustrating…"

After Second Lieutenant Perschmann (melissa, Team Leaf, 3-16) shot her in a theatrical manner, Siri (bergamot, Team Fruit, 4-23) stomped on the ground bitterly.

And so, many of the participants ended up confused, and this abnormal training drill continued.

The maneuvering grounds were styled after the Federacy's unique winding urban environment, and turning a corner could lead to you running into the scent of a different perfume. It was so that Eugene discovered a scent rather different from his aniseed perfume's warm, heavy fragrance. It was the cool fragrance of winter conifer trees.

He took a step forward with his gun drawn. Shin instantly reacted, turning his own muzzle at Eugene, but then his eyes widened and he froze up.

"Eugene, wai—"

"Sorry, but I'm not waiting! Prepare yourself!" Eugene pulled the trigger, raising his voice in an attempt at a cool battle cry.

Everyone in this exercise were given paintball guns fashioned after their usual firearms. Eugene's didn't have a firing hammer, so it wouldn't get caught when pulled out, and instead had an internal striker. Eugene's 9 mm Federacy standard issue pistol spewed out a paintball which hit Shin dead on, covering him in color. Seeing Shin with his head covered in paint, Eugene puffed up his chest.

"You thought I was on your side because of my name tag, didn't you? We're both red, and my number is 5-20, so it's close to your 5-19."

Shin's tag was 5-19, while Eugene's was just one off at 5-20... meaning their birthdays were respectively May 19th and 20th. Quite the coincidence.

Shin, however, regarded him with an incredulous expression as he wiped away the paint smeared over him.

"I didn't mean that..."

"You're out, big bro!" Came an unexpected verdict from the spectator seats.

The one to offer that cruelly delighted commentary was Nina (smell of spa, tag number 3-8 with an extra rabbit appliqué).

"Huh... Why?!" Eugene was stunned. "My bullet hit him, not the other way around!"

"That was friendly fire, Eugene... Hitting someone on your side disqualifies you," Shin said gently.

This only confused Eugene further. "Friendly fire...? But Shin, your perfume smells like leaves. You said it's temple juniper, right? And mine is aniseed, so it's fruit. How would this be friendly fire...?"

Shin scratched his paint-splotched cheek uncomfortably. The colors of each participant's paintball matched their number tag's, meaning Eugene's was red and Shin looked all bloodied... Or rather, not really, since the paint was much too transparent to come off as blood. It looked more like he was covered in strawberry jam.

"You know what I found out only during this exercise...?"

"What?"

"Temple juniper. And, you know, juniper berries."

"Well, yeah..."

"...Juniper *berries.*"

"Ah."

Eugene exclaimed in realization, and Shin nodded. Despite smelling like conifer trees...

"Temple juniper extract comes from fruit."

Standing frozen in a standoff were Anette (tag 11-12) gripping her Republic standard issue automatic pistol with both hands, and Kaie (tag 4-7) holding her own pistol with one hand.

"H-hold on, Kaie, you're...Team Flower, right?! That smells like jasmine, right?"

"Indeed, Arabian jasmine... They call it Sambac jasmine. And you're...what, Annette? I can tell it's floral."

"Lily of the valley, it's lily of the valley! We're both Team Flower, don't shoot!"

After some initial prattling, the two ended up teaming up together.

"I think we can safely assume That team Flower's opponents are basically the boys?" Kaie pondered.

"Fundamentally speaking, yes, but...Captain Olivia got hit with friendly fire because of that earlier." Annette said with a shrug.

"Oh, yeah, the captain has rose perfume... But rose is the easiest flower to recognize, how did someone from Team Flower get it wrong and fire at him?"

"Well, brace yourself for this one... It was Lena's dad."

"Huh...?"

He was also Team Flower (sweet acacia, Team Flower, tag 5-3, uses the same perfume as his wife, Margareta, who isn't participating in this drill), and somehow insisted that "there can't be boys in Team Flower!" and used that faulty logic to fire at Olivia (Rose de Mai, Team Flower, tag 3-8), which got them both disqualified.

This logic was entirely wrong, of course, as the head of the Reginleif research team (who was already disqualified) had geranium perfume, and even Brigadier General Karlstahl was Team Flower with his magnolia perfume, so apparently plenty of men used floral cologne.

"...Hm. I suppose you two are my deputy and adjutant. It makes sense that you would know what ingredients your liege's cologne would be..."

Shifting his gun—a machine pistol used by United Kingdom special forces—selector to full auto, Vika (olibanum, Team Sparkles, tag 12-22) dangled the weapon from his finger by the trigger guard and shrugged. It was a refined gesture made less graceful due to the fact that his face and top were spotted with blue and white paint.

A machine pistol was capable of full-auto firing, meant for sweeping through large groups of enemies at once. But since his opponents opened fire on him without any need to distinguish between friend and foe—in other words, without needing to smell his cologne—he ended up getting hit before he could even pull the trigger.

Casting a sidelong glance at the attackers that eliminated him, Vika frowned. The fact that they shot him without any mercy whatsoever was a little rattling even for him.

"Quite merciless of you, though."

"Would you expect anything else?"

"Since this is a match, I surmised going easy on you would be discourteous of me." Zashya (neroli, Team Flower, tag 4-2) replied calmly, to which Lerche (helichrysum, team Flower, tag 9-3) nodded solemnly. Both of them were holding the United Kingdom's standard issue 7.62 automatic pistol, infamous for not having a manual safety.

Participants freezing up, aiming their guns at each other, and only then pausing to take in the fragrance of the other's perfume to distinguish which team they were on was a common sight in this exercise.

Just like that, Daiya (tag 9-16), exclaimed and lowered his gun, while Theo (tag 4-20) lowered his gun while remaining cautious. If

Theo's bitter orange perfume got Daiya to halt his attack, he was likely Team Fruit, too.

Sniffing the air, he caught a whiff of his fragrance. It was the scent of summer fruit, full of the refreshing scent of greenery packed with moisture… Melon, or watermelon, to be exact.

"…Daiya, is your perfume melon?"

Daiya looked bashful for some reason. "Uh, no, I'm… Uh, I'm Mr. Aquanaut."

"That was you?!" Theo shouted despite himself.

But indeed, that was the kind of scent that suited Daiya. Summery, but reminiscent of water. Plus, it fitted Anju's lotus perfume.

"And Anju already got taken out, so…as fellow members of Team Fruit, let's take revenge for her, okay?"

Theo's lips curled up into a smile. Anju was Team Flower, meaning she was their enemy in this exercise. But still.

"Yeah, we can get revenge for her."

This whole exercise was a joke, after all.

Looking around, he caught a flash of that abominable scarlet hair. Having given up on trying to distinguish allies by their scent, Kiriya (tag 7-22, tag color red) opened fire instantly. Perhaps predicting that his opponent would be careless enough to instantly open fire, Gilwiese (tag 12-1, for some reason he was the only one with a black name tag) dodged the shot, evading the surprise attack.

He dived behind a wall the paintball couldn't possibly penetrate for cover, and then peeked out of its shadow and shouted. The Brantolote archduchy abhorred the idea of using the same kind of pistol as the Onyx, and had specially engraved 7.62 mm pistols made for their subordinates.

"Look, I understand you hate me for being a subordinate of the Brantolotes, but at least try to follow the exercise's rules, Kiriya Nouzen! At least check if I'm on your side or not before you shoot!"

Hearing this, Kiriya finally recognized the man's fragrance.

"...Musk. You're Team Sparkles, meaning you're my enemy. I was right to shoot you, after all."

Incidentally, Kiriya's perfume was cedarwood, in other words, Team Leaf. Like he said, the two were opponents, but even on the off chance they were on the same team, Kiriya was very much intent on taking Gilwiese out. House Brantolote were the Nouzen Clan's mortal enemies, after all, and moreover, Archduchess Brantolote was a major threat to his empress, Frederica's, sovereignty.

Gilwiese clicked his tongue loudly. This was why those combat-crazy Nouzen conquerors were so difficult to deal with.

"I suppose in the end, a lowly knight who only gets to wear the name Nouzen out of pity is undisciplined even among a family of rabid dogs."

Kiriya scoffed at him with a cold smile. "No matter how much you like licking the boots of your master, you can't even get yourself to earn that bit of pity, mongrel."

"..."

Their exchange of hostility sizzled up to the point where there was no more need for words. The crimson and ebony knights clashed.

"Whoa...!"

"Oh...!"

Spotting a petite, blond girl, Hilnå—Isuka (tag 2-4) was distracted and lowered his gun. If it was the battlefield, it'd be one thing, but this was an exercise and a game of pretend, so he couldn't very well fire on a child.

Hilnå (tag 6-27), on the other hand, looked at him, her clear golden eyes open wide.

"This fragrance... Is it rosemary? Then you're Team Leaf, same as me?"

"Huh? You're Team Leaf, too?"

Isuka unfortunately couldn't guess what the fragrance wafting up from Hilnå was. Hilnå nodded in affirmation. True to her statement that they were in the same team, she lowered her gun, a magnum auto (an engraved model for 357 magnum rounds) that was much too large and boorish for her dainty hands.

"Yes. My perfume is aloeswood, meaning it's taken from a tree. So, if you don't mind...could we cooperate? Despite appearances, I am a general, so I can guarantee I won't slow you down."

Isuka looked up tiredly. Babysitting wasn't something he'd be good at.

"...Yes, well. I guess I wouldn't sleep well at night if I just said no."

Plus, there were two idiots fighting savagely without regard for the exercise, too.

"Really, though. Those fools Kiriya and Gilwiese are going too far."

"Pardon our reckless child for being so absurd... Anyway, take it away, First Lieutenant Aldrecht, operator of the maneuvering grounds' special traps."

"I swear, everything goes in this exercise..."

At Joschka and Yatrai's prodding, Aldrecht (origanum, Team Leaf, tag 1-13) cradled his forehead in frustration. Meanwhile, Prince Zafar walked over with Nina riding on his shoulders. The little girl waved at Aldrecht, to which he raised a hand and pushed the button right in front of him.

Suddenly, as Kiriya and Gilwiese were grappling (having thrown away their guns and resorted to hand-to-hand combat), the ground under their feet suddenly opened up.

The two looked down in shock, having just enough time to scream before they plummeted into the abyss and were removed from the running.

Walking into a flagstone intersection from a side road with heavy, shambling steps no one would ever fail to recognize, was Fido. Even during this exercise, it served its role of supplying and picking up trash.

Haruto's (lime, Team Fruit, tag 7-4) eyes flicked in his direction before he once again looked forward. But then he paused, hummed in suspicion, and turned his eyes back to Fido. For some reason, the smell of its machine oil struck him as oddly fragrant.

"...Fido?"

"*Pi.*"

"Are you participating in the drill, too?"

"*Pi!*"

Its machine oil had the fragrance of tropical mango and coconuts. Seeing the Scavenger thrust one of its machine arms up toward the sky in what looked like a salute, Haruto exhaled in relief. That was close. It all turned out okay because they were both on Team Fruit, but if it wasn't, he'd have been defenseless and vulnerable. He wouldn't have expected Fido to be part of the exercise.

On closer inspection, the container Fido was carrying on his back was loaded with buckets full of paint, which was apparently Fido's means of offense. The quantity of paint in those buckets was quite extreme.

"I see... So that's why they let Team Flower have so many members without adjusting the numbers. Having Shin on our team along with you means Team Fruit is really strong."

"*Pi!*" Fido replied, in a manner that seemed to suggest it was saying *You can count on me!*

But then Haruto came to a certain ominous realization. If this was how the team division worked, that would mean the smallest team...

"...Team Sparkles must have some really dangerous people."

And honestly, all the members of Team Sparkles were powerhouses.

"Even if it is an exercise, how long has it been since I faced you on the battlefield like this, Yuuna...? I love you with all my heart, but under the Nouzen name, I can't show any mercy on the field of battle!"

"Of course not, Reisha. I'll show you the power of the Maika Witch!"

Facing his wife, Yuuna (orchid, Team Flower, tag 1-2), on the battlefield, only for the two to take each other out at the same time, was Reisha (ambergris, Sparkles, tag 6-14), the eldest son of the Nouzen clan, the once-leading warrior house of the Empire.

"It's you, Willem… Please don't let your immaturity emerge at times like these."

"I considered letting you take the win…but as a former armored infantryman, I can't afford to lose to a tank woman when it comes to melee combat."

Grethe (mimosa, Team Flower, tag 8-11) grumbled as she sat, covered head to toe in paint, as Willem (labdanum, Sparkles, tag 2-16) offered her a hand without even a single splotch of paint on him. His reputation of being a monstrous armored infantryman who cut down Legion in melee combat was in full, vivid display on this oddly pointless occasion.

Grethe took his hand, intentionally smearing his white gloves with sticky paint, and furrowed her brows.

"By the way, are you using a standard issue pistol? I'm surprised you didn't mind a small handgun with low capacity."

Willm shrugged. The pistol's range, power and accuracy were low, meaning it was inadequate to serve as a main armament in modern warfare.

"It just needs to do the bare minimum. Being picky about it would just be a waste of time… If anything, I have to ask why you're using a non-military pistol—"

He paused. Grethe was glaring at him.

"A waste of time?! Don't you think that if you have to use a gun, you'd be better off using a good one…? Now listen here, this gun has a unique gas lock breech system and a cutting-edge squeeze cocker to increase its rapid-fire functionality—"

"Fine, fine, I was wrong, just stop chanting your black magic at me."

And finally, there was this guy.

"Wait, young Raiden Shuga! I know you've been looking after Shin, but that's of no consequence right now! Let's have a match, fair and square! You, too, Dustin Jaegar, Erwin Marcel, and Canaan Nyuud! I'll take you on, too!"

"Dha-ha-ha! I've been waiting for this, Raiden and the other three! You, too, Bernholdt and old Ishmael!"

"That's right, dear brother! How can we have a match if you keep running!"

"Shiden and Colonel Esther is one thing, but I'm not picking a fight with the Priest! I'm running!"

Toting a 45 caliber single-action pistol—the Republic Military's first generation standard issue weapon—the Priest (myrrh, Team Sparkles, tag 10-10), with his grizzly bear physique, barreled across the maneuvering grounds like a rampaging bull on a rodeo, with Shiden (birch-tar oil, Team Sparkles, tag 6-18) and Esther (elemi, Team Sparkles, tag 7-6) following behind him.

They were pursuing Raiden (cypress, tag 8-25), Dustin (pine needle, tag 3-19), Marcel (marjoram, tag 9-9), Canaan (patchouli, tag 8-18), Bernholdt (tobacco, tag 1-16), and Ishmael (bay laurel, tag 8-12, everyone from Raiden to him being Team Leaf), cutting down whoever couldn't run fast enough, one by one.

The first to fall were Dustin, who ran out of stamina; and Marcel who wasn't a combatant; followed by Noele and Mele (both were marigold, Team Flower, tag 4-27 and tag 1-12 respectively), as well as Ninha (genet, Team Flower, tag 6-5) who were unlucky enough to pass by.

"Uwaaaaah?!"

"Gaaaaaaaaah?!"

"Aaaaaaah?!"

"Did we just get someone by mistake?!"

"The Priest just sent three people flying…and he's not slowing down…!"

"I reckon if you throw the Reverend at a Leviathan, he'd probably come out on top! What the hell, he's the ultimate weapon!"

As Dustin and Marcel watched in horror as the trio went flying with a scream. Canaan, Bernholdt, and Ishmael grumbled, but the Priest showed no sign of stopping. None of them could fix their guns at him—not Canaan and Raiden, not Ishmael—with his 9 mm small pistol, which wouldn't be useful in a naval battle against a Leviathan—or Bernholdt, who had the highly dependable, large, boorish, Vargus-constructed pistol he used for decades.

The green, refreshing and stimulating scent of conifer trees was being drowned out by the scent of myrrh, and everyone was powerless to stop it.

"...Does that mean Team Leaf is basically wiped out?"

"Isuka and Hilnå are from Team Leaf and they're about to get cornered, too."

Alice (narcissus, Team Flower, tag 4-18) and Suiu (hyacinth, Team Flower, tag 12-13) described the situation as they watched the Priest and his two partners continue their massacre, and Haruto and Fido pursued Isuka and Hilnå in another part of the grounds (impressively enough, Isuka picked up the slow Hilnå and carried her like a piece of luggage as he fled). Zelene (tuberose, tag 12-9) and Touka (honeysuckle, Team Flower, tag 8-31), who were allied with the other two, watched with horrified expressions as Team Leaf was thoroughly beaten.

Out of everyone in the sweetly fragranced Team Flower, this was a group of especially dazzling white flowers.

As an aside, much like how Rei, Kiriya, Aldrecht, and Václav weren't in the Dinosauria or Morpho forms, Zelene was showing off her human form for the first time in the series. She was a Pyrope with long crimson hair, a slender physique, and very gentle eyes.

By the way, Haruto wasn't as adamant, but Fido was chasing Isuka with clear animosity for some reason, which made Isuka extra desperate.

"Wait, stop! That's dangerous! Hold up, dammit! What did I even do to this Scavenger?!"

"*Piiiii! Pipipiiii!*"

As Fido let out a sequence of loud beeps that probably stood for shouting, Zelene frowned.

"It's saying 'You know what you did,' I think."

Touka nodded beside her. She wasn't sure why she thought this way, but...

"What a coincidence. I got the impression it said the same thing."

* * *

"...You know, thinking about it, if we just lay low, we can't really lose."

"I mean, the Reverend's a weapon of indiscriminate destruction... If he spots Team Flower or Team Fruit, he just goes at 'em."

Like Yuuto (sandalwood, tag 1-27) and Guren (rosewood, tag 11-22)—who were both teamed up as members of Team Leaf—said, the Priest chased down Theo and Daiya from Team Fruit earlier (which got Esther disqualified) and was currently pursuing Team Flower's Olivia and Zashya, as well as Svenja, who was being carried screaming in Olivia's arms. Meanwhile, Lerche boldly stood guard and took out Shiden, only to be effortlessly blown away by the Priest.

Yuuto was accompanied by the old lady who was Raiden's teacher (spikenard, Team Leaf, tag 5-1) and Chitori (lavender, which was drawn from herbs, making her Team Leaf and not Flower, tag 10-5). Having to escort two noncombatants made it difficult for him to fight back, and so he chose to lie in wait. He had no intention of getting covered in paint for this absurd exercise.

Lieutenant Colonel Mialona (carnation, Team Flower, tag 3-31), who took this absurd exercise quite seriously, charged in against two opponents despite being outnumbered—albeit, they were noncombatants—only to be gunned down.

"Mhm, this coldheadedness is refreshing. That's what I'd expect out of the Eighty-Six!" She said, flashing a thumbs-up. "Don't let anyone call you cowards, Second Lieutenant Yuuto, Sergeant Guren!"

"Leave me alone."

"Besides, we shot you down, could you at least take it seriously and pretend to be dead?"

In the end, the Priest went up against his teammate Kujo (tolu balsam, Team Sparkles, tag 3-17), successfully beating him, only to be disqualified for friendly fire.

* * *

And so.

"I get that this whole exercise is over-the-top, but you don't have to put up this weird act."

As the sole survivors of Team Fruit and Flower respectively, there were no more footsteps or shots fired as Shin and Lena stood there, facing off in the paint-covered maneuvering grounds. As Shin spoke, his eyes narrowed sarcastically, Lena went red in the face over getting carried away.

"Sh-shut up! We're opponents in this exercise! Let's fight, fair and square!"

Even with all that bravado thrown his way, Shin wasn't inclined to shoot her, even for an exercise. At the same time, he knew Lena would be upset if he took it easy on her. As he held his pistol in hand, not budging an inch, he tried to figure out how to go about this.

"Yes. You're a member of Team Fruit and our opponent. And this is a match."

But, in the next moment, a shower of paint splashed over them from the side.

Lena and Shin, taken by surprise, turned to look. With his body already covered in red from Eugen's friendly fire, the green paint spilled over him resulting in a nasty mixture of paint. A figure emerged from behind a building, throwing away a bucket of paint—a tall Republic officer with a scar on his face. Karlstahl.

"Carelessness is a liability, Captain Nouzen, last member of Team Fruit."

It wasn't clear who had been able to defeat Fido, considering it was a ten-tonne heavy machine, but apparently someone had. Shin was the last remaining member of Team Fruit, and he was just disqualified. Team Sparkles and Team Leaf were already wiped out, leaving only Lena from Team Flower.

Lena blinked in amazement.

"...Oh. That's right, Uncle. You use magnolia cologne."

"Indeed… Victory is ours, Lena. And everyone else lost, the captain there included."

Karlstahl (white magnolia, Flower, tag 11-27) was also part of her team. Seeing his proud declaration, Shin fell to his knees despite himself. He wasn't going to deny being careless, but really, does this make sense as a conclusion? Does losing like this count?

Karlstahl looked down on Shin and spoke with a smirk. He wanted to say this for some time now, and the right man to say it ended up disqualifying himself much earlier.

"I'm not giving you my daughter, hooligan. Pathetic loser."

"Kuh…!"

Incensed by the statement, Shin grit his teeth bitterly.

On the other side of the grounds, Václav shouted, "Wait, Jérôme, that's my line!", but sadly his voice didn't reach Shin's ears…

86

EIGHTY-SIX

AFTERWORD

Thank you, dear readers, as always. This is Asato Asato. The series' second short story anthology, *86 Alter.1* "Youth with a Hint of the Reaper", is published for your reading pleasure!

This volume gathers the first to sixth volume's store and fair exclusive side stories, detailing moments from Shin and his friends' daily lives between the age of twelve and the autumn after he turned eighteen, published in chronological order within the story's timeline. I included the long version of "Star Shower Lemonade," as the published version had to be shortened due to page number limitations. It also compiles some unpublished short stories, so anyone who hasn't read these exclusive stories can enjoy the full package!

In place of our usual analysis, here's some commentary about the unpublished and newly written stories!

"Lena+Annette," "Theo+Kaie+Haurto+Fido," and "Meanwhile, Annette and Dustin…"

These are three unpublished store exclusive stories. For the store exclusives for Volumes 1-6, I made to write the necessary number of stories plus an extra two (I wrote them under the pretense of backup in case a story gets voted out, but I basically just wrote whatever I wanted). Any unused stories were typically published on Kakuyomu, but these three ended up timed poorly and weren't published anywhere. "Lena+Annette" and "Theo+Kaie+Haruto+Fido" were written as exclusive side stories for Volume 1, meaning I wrote them six years ago! That really takes me back…

* * *

"October 2nd (Anju's Birthday)" and "November 12th (Annette's Birthday)"

These are newly written stories.

For these two (along with Vika and Frederica), I haven't been able to write their birthday chapters for Kakuyomu, since the story's timeline hadn't reached October and November yet. Ep. 11 takes place in October, while Ep. 12 takes place in November, so I finally managed to write chapters for those two. I'll definitely try to write the chapters for Vika, who has a December birthday, and Frederica, who has a February birthday!

"All-Star Perfume Battle"

People were curious! They wanted to know all the characters' birthdays, perfumes, and—perhaps most importantly—what pistols each faction in the story uses, so I mixed it all into this comprehensive side story.

Getting all the characters to appear meant the timeline had to be toyed with, so you can feel free to think of this as not an actual event that took place, but some kind of mass hallucination Shin and his friends experienced (after all, Rei, Kaie, and Eugene are already dead…).

By the way, characters like Grandpa Seiei, Grandma Gelda, Vika's father, Auntie Svetlana, and Lieutenant General Bel Aegis all share their perfumes with their successors; respectively Reisha and Yatrai, Yuuna, Zafar, Vika, and Olivia. For this reason, they weren't featured.

Also, the Alliance's standard issue pistol wasn't shown, given that Olivia was accidentally shot at and chased down by Václav and the Priest, so I'll write its details here:

"A highly accurate but rather expensive-looking for military purposes 9 mm single-stack automatic pistol."

Lastly, some thanks.

To my editors, Tabata and Nishimura. I'm glad you laughed when you heard the idea of the birthday tags and tropical Fido.

To Shirabii. Lena's troubled expression on the Volume 12 cover was lovely in its own way, but seeing her carefree smile on this volume's cover is a pleasure. I wish she could smile like this all the time during the main story, too…!

To I-IV, who burst out laughing at the idea of Fido taking part in the all-star battle, swinging buckets around! Thank you for designing the galactic cruiser and the staves for the magical girl spinoff, too!

To Somemiya. The *Magical Girl Regina ★ Lena* is beginning its manga adaptation! Lena and Annette's magical girl forms in the first volume are so pretty, and the Eighty-Six characters are adorable with their little doggy ears! Plus, the three old military officers are so pitiful. It's great!

And of course, to all the readers who read this far. The Reaper and the Bloodstained Queen have their moments of youth every so often—or rather, more often than not—but I hope you enjoy watching them and their friends grow and mature.

In any case, I hope that, for even a short moment, I could take you all to a happy get-together in the Spearhead squadron's base, and to the cheer and clamor of the days in Rüstkammer base.